The Girls of Fall

Jessica Minyard

CENTURION
BOOKS

Centurion Books

THE GIRLS OF FALL © 2021 by Jessica Minyard

All Rights Reserved

First Edition. November 2021

Published by Centurion Books

www.jessicaminyard.com

ISBN: 978-1-957004-00-6

eBook ISBN: 978-1-957004-01-3

Cover by The Red Leaf Book Design

Also by Jessica Minyard

The Littlest Dragon

Fat Girl Love Story: Poems

Nonnatus: Poems

This book contains material that may be triggering to some readers, including: sex (fade-to-black, implied), discussions of sex, language, mild drug use, mild alcohol use, alcoholism, sudden character death (off-page), religion, and discussions of religion.

To the messy girls, with wild hearts and curly hair

ONE

August 2005

FATHER ADRIAN WAS A sex god. The Adonis of holy men. He had thick auburn hair that fell into his eyes and the broad-shouldered, thin-waisted body of someone who used to play quarterback before he decided to devote his life to Jesus. Standing behind the altar, he held aloft the body of Christ in a golden bowl.

It was a Wednesday, which meant chapel for the first two periods. As always, chapel was divided equally into boys and girls—boys in the back pews and girls in the front. They didn't trust us to not tempt the boys with our womanly wiles, I guess. This suited us fine because we enjoyed the unobstructed view of Father Adrian unless we got stuck behind one of the huge white columns. Chapel was optional, but attendance had definitely increased since Father Adrian showed up at the end of the last school year. If you didn't go to chapel, you had to go to class, and ogling Father Adrian was definitely the better choice.

I glanced over at Bridget, whose attention was focused on her lap. She sat with her legs crossed, her phone hidden by skirt and thigh, an outrageously pink fingernail flitting over the keyboard.

"Would you screw Father Adrian?" I asked her, attempting to keep my lips from moving too much.

She looked up at Father Adrian stepping down from the altar with the Eucharistic Ministers in tow and gave him a long, leisurely look. "Probably."

"Me too."

In addition to being rather drool-inducing, Father Adrian smiled easily and liked to crack jokes during his homily, much to the annoyance of the only, and elderly, sister present.

Bridget resumed her furious texting. From what I could glimpse, there were a lot of "fuck yous" being exchanged. With her head bowed like that and her face scrunched up, she appeared particularly devout. We hadn't even made it through the first week of school yet, and already the drama had begun.

I poked Bridget in the ribs. "Nun."

The phone was snapped shut and covered with clasped hands as Sister Constance patrolled past our pew on her ever-vigilant hunt for evildoers. She paused briefly before moving on, and I resumed my lewd doodle in the margins of my hymnal.

By the time chapel ended, it was time for third period. Devotional Studies—joy of my life. I heard rumors that kids in public school got to pick their electives, but in here, we had to make room on our schedules every year for Devotional Studies.

Bridget and I walked together, as always, a gaggle of classmates and wannabes trailing behind us. You see, I held a coveted position in Saint Agnes High School's social hierarchy: Bridget Margaret James's Best Friend.

I first met Bridget in Sunday school when she had blond pigtails with pink bows. She took one look at me, and her big blue eyes sparkled as if to say, you, friend. Then she ran over and grabbed my hand and announced that we were now best friends. Since we had just moved to the district specifically so my mom could send me to Catholic school, I wasn't complaining about effortlessly making my first friend.

On the outside, we looked like disparate girls, and I'm sure some people wondered how we stayed friends. Bridget was naturally popular, and I was the quiet one; she just got blonder and slender and grew soft curves while I was the curly brunette who just got thicker around the bottom half; her parents could pay tuition out of pocket, and I was on half scholarship and the other half reduced tuition because I only had a one-parent household.

We weren't supposed to wear jewelry to school, but we each had a black elastic choker on, hidden by the collars of our polos. Each choker had half a silver heart charm. Mine said Best and hers said Friend. We had bought them together in Florida the summer after my dad left. Mom let me go on vacation with the Jameses so I wouldn't hear her crying in her room. She needed me out of the house as much as I needed to lose myself in cutoffs, sun, sand, and virgin margaritas, my partner in crime leading the way.

Now juniors, the only class we had together this semester was Devotional Studies. I was on the Art and French track, and she was on the Economics and Spanish track; our paths wouldn't meet again until AP U.S. History next year.

We sat together behind Zack Werwie and Corion Jump. Corion used to bring condoms to class and blow them up like party balloons until Sister Constance finally caught him. She smacked him with a ruler, threw a right medieval fit, and banished him to the principal's office. Nobody knew what happened after that, and nobody was brave enough to ask. Corion never brought condoms to class again, though.

Sister Constance swept around the silent room, the stench of old mothballs trailing along behind her, throwing our journals down on the desks. Every day of every year, we were given a prompt and had the first fifteen minutes of class to work on it. I flipped to yesterday:

Saints are holy people and human people who lived extraordinary lives. Each saint the Church honors responded to God's invitation to use his or her unique gifts. God calls each one of us to be a saint. In two paragraphs, explain how God calls you to use your own gifts.

Under this super compelling prompt, I had drawn a detailed picture of a zombie—replete with gore and dripping brains—along with an elaborate illustration of my name. Obviously, Sister Constance was unhappy with my answer because, under my drawing, she had scribbled a big red F and a frowny face.

"That's disgusting." Bridget was looking at my drawing with an arched eyebrow and pursed lips.

Bridget's journal was spread open, so everyone could see the A stamped under at least three paragraphs of her tiny handwriting. Nobody could have that many gifts.

"You don't even try," she said, fingers trailing into her polo to rub the choker. She did that sometimes when she was especially exasperated with me as if she could transmute her thoughts through touch.

I didn't respond. I just opened my journal to a fresh page and waited for Sister Constance to dish out today's prompt. She stood at the front of the room, dressed all in dismal gray, smiling. It was never a good sign when a nun was smiling.

"Class," she said, "today we are going to have a guest speaker. Please welcome Sister Francis from Sisters of Mercy."

Obligatory applause ensued, and all heads turned to the back of the room where Sister Francis was standing. The sister was petite with short blond hair and a sweet face, but looks could be deceiving, especially when it came to nuns.

"But before we begin, I ask that these students wait out in the hallway." Sister Constance started reading off names from her grade book. I was surprised when she called my name but not unduly worried. I gathered my stuff and followed the other six out of the classroom. What good little sheep we were.

I was just about to take my seat up against the wall with them when Sister Constance poked her head out the door.

"Sophia." She beckoned me to join her in the doorway. She glared at me over her long nose for so long, I started to fidget. "This is a Call to Vocation, and we do not think you possess the qualities we are looking for in those who wish to join our order." She paused again. "That being said, I would like for you to do something productive with your time. Take this to Father Adrian." She handed me a small white envelope. That's when she spied the notebook I had clutched to my chest and snatched it out of my hands. "And you know journals do not leave the classroom." She slammed the door.

I finally noticed I was the only girl asked to leave the classroom for the nun-recruiting event.

That was depressing. Here I was, under the impression convents would take anyone brave enough to volunteer, when in fact, there were certain qualities one had to have. I started walking down the hallway, acutely aware of the six pairs of boy eyes fixated on the backs of my thighs, turning the envelope over in my hands. It wasn't addressed but had Sister Constance's signature scrawled across the seal. I was intrigued.

The walk was short, and soon I found myself standing in the doorway of the parish office. Father Adrian was leaning against a set of morose gray filing cabinets, flipping through a manila folder. He was wearing his black cassock, which was quite attractive against his fair skin. He appeared thoroughly engrossed in whatever he was reading, so I attempted to clear my throat delicately. I ended up choking.

Father Adrian looked up. "Do you need some water?"

I dismissed this notion with a wave and continued coughing violently into my elbow. After a few painful seconds, I was able to regain whatever dignity I still had left and looked up.

Father Adrian put away his folder and sat down behind the desk. He gestured for me to sit in one of the fancy leather chairs opposite him. "Do you need to make a confession?"

Forgive me, Father, for I have sinned. It has been 365 days since my last confession. I'm having impure thoughts about my priest. "No."

He smiled. Two dimples appeared on his otherwise unmarked face. His front two teeth slightly overlapped, which caused him to appear much too young and not like the learned holy man he was masquerading as.

"They're doing a Call to Vocation in class," I said.

"Ah."

"Sister Constance kicked me out. She wanted me to give you this." I passed the envelope over the desk. He opened it deftly and scanned the brief letter.

"So you're one of those." He leaned back in his chair, crossed his legs, and rested one hand on his knee, the letter dangling loosely from his fingers. "One of the many misguided youth Sister Constance likes to send me."

"I'm not misguided." I wasn't, really. I made decent grades, played varsity soccer, and spoke passable French. I wasn't in line for valedictorian (solid number seven for three years), wasn't the team captain, and a Frenchman would laugh at my pronunciation, but I didn't think that qualified me as misguided.

He smiled again, and I forgot what else I was going to say. "You're Sophia?"

"Yes." I spoke to my knees. Oh, be still my beating heart!

"Sister Constance is worried that your behavior in class might be—"

"That's about me?" I nodded toward the letter he still held.

"Sister Constance seems to think you're acting out." My leg started bouncing. "How're things at home?" That old witch sent me to get counseling. "Any problems with your peers?" She probably thought talking to Father Adrian would lead me to the path of righteousness. Yeah. "How're your classes?"

"Fine, fine, and fine. Everything's fine. Listen, Father, I don't know what Sister Constance said, but I don't need any help."

He held the letter up and cleared his throat. "Let's see. 'Miss Salvatore is a menace to my classroom and a disturbance to my other pupils. She frequently speaks out of turn, shows a blatant disregard for authority, performs poorly on her assignments, and makes a general mockery of such a fine establishment for the Lord.' Are you mocking the Lord's establishment, Sophia?" The corners of his bright eyes crinkled in amusement.

"I would never do such a thing, Father." That was a lie, I probably would, but never in front of Sister Constance for fear she would smite me.

"So, what did you do?"

I told him about the prompts and journals and my latest artistic response.

"I would like to see that," he said.

"We're not allowed to take our journals out of class."

"I'll just have to ask her if I can see yours to investigate such a serious allegation." He waved the letter around.

"She hates me."

"I'm sure she doesn't." We both looked at the letter, and I knew he was thinking the same thing I was: Yeah, right.

The bell rang for fourth period, and I jumped. "Um...I've got to go. Class."

I stood up, and so did he, walking around the desk to clasp my hand in both of his. "It was nice to see you,

Sophia. Feel free to come back anytime if you need to talk."
His hands were warm, and my skin hummed at the
contact.

I could feel heat creeping up my neck and just nodded,
not trusting my mouth to say something smooth and not
horribly embarrass me...again.

After Art and lunch, my next class was Earth Science since I
flat-out refused to be on track for AP Bio or Chem.

Mrs. Conway was a beanpole of a woman with close-
cropped hair and severe bangs that tended to be on the
frizzy side. She wore long, graphic skirts and clogs and
would stand at the door greeting everyone until the final
bell rang. I entered the classroom and went straight to my
preferred spot: somewhere in the middle but definitely in
the very back row. I slid into the desk and shoved my
backpack under the desk between my legs.

The class filled up quickly, and I wasn't alone in the
back row for long. Rafael Esparza slid into the desk to my
right with no backpack and just a beat-up notebook he
flopped on the top. "Got an extra pen, Salvatore?" he
drawled.

I rolled my eyes. Rafael Esparza had been haunting me
ever since he got his hooks into Bridget in middle school.

They were no high school Romeo and Juliet; they were on-again and off-again like a light switch. I couldn't decide if it was his personality that bothered me or the fact that he was the reason my best friend was never single. I would literally bet my life that he was on the receiving end of Bridget's furious text barrage earlier.

Rafael was attractive in a scrubby way that was very annoying. His tie was loose and askew, polo unbuttoned, green Saint Agnes cardigan sleeves cuffed messily. His dark hair was effortlessly feathery and came to his chin.

"Not one for you, *Rafi*."

His dark green eyes narrowed. Rafi was a pet name I had heard his abuela throw at him one day in the school parking lot. It was not a name he boasted at school. He slouched back in his chair.

I smirked. This round was mine.

Right before the final bell rang to signal class beginning, in strolled London Hart, his uniform as crisp as Rafael's was sloppy. My pencil stopped its aimless scratching. London hadn't been in this class earlier in the week; I would have *definitely* noticed. He must have switched his schedule for some unfathomable reason.

London had grown up over the summer.

He was taller than I remembered and shoulders broader. Everything was thicker—neck, arms, and thighs—like he had been inflated by puberty. London was Saint Aggie's quarterback, or he would be after Craig Bishop graduated in May. Right now, he was only second-half, but everyone knew he was heir to the position.

My mouth must have been hanging open because I heard, "See something you like?" soft and low next to my ear. Rafael had leaned over the aisle and was right up in my personal space.

It took all my self-control not to stab him with a pencil.

London did this weird combination of secret handshakes and side-hugs with three other football players who were taking up the front row before taking his seat. But not before I noticed how snug his khakis were.

Mrs. Conway clapped her hands, brightly chiming, "Welcome to another beautiful day, intrepid learners!"

Rafael had thankfully retreated to his space when Conway started writing the day's agenda on the whiteboard and humming tunelessly while she worked.

I flipped to an empty page in my sketchbook and started taking notes.

Junior year. Goal: finally get boyfriend.
Make all other friends jealous. LH????

And then I started penciling in his face, the sweet music of the graphite scratching the thick paper raising the hair on my arms.

A new school year was always bittersweet because my birthday always seemed to fall the week before. My mom had come through with a lime green second-gen iPod mini, and I had spent the last week of my summer break uploading my vast CD collection to iTunes. We weren't allowed to have music players during class time, but I had the iPod peeking out of my skirt pocket anyway so that everyone could see I had finally ditched the Walkman.

This year I turned seventeen, which was one of those uneventful birthdays. I already had my license and was legally allowed on the road, but I still wasn't old enough to buy anything fun like cigarettes or porn. Not that I would ever smoke because I was a varsity athlete, and our coach would murder me. And I was seventeen and had never had a boyfriend. This one boy had kissed me on the cheek and stolen my chips in middle school, but I don't think he counted.

Seventeen was old enough.

Bridget had already changed into her soccer uniform and was slipping the black and white captain's band over her shin guards when I finally made it to the locker room after school. It was unprecedented that a junior would have the position, but our team had spoken.

She cornered me at my locker. "Where've you been?"

"I got held late after seventh."

She gibbered at me while I changed. "Rafael and I broke up again today."

"Yeah?" For the third time. This week.

"He's an ass. What do you think about Zack?"

"Zack's good." He liked video games and held the door open. I was pretty sure he was Agnostic. Rafael was a social enigma. Didn't play any sports but was friends with all the jocks. Was a consummate underachiever but dated the girl who was at the top of our class. Zack would be the white boy to annoy Rafael the most.

"So, where'd you go during Devotional Studies?"

I shoved my school uniform and backpack into the maw of the locker and slammed the door. "Got sent to Father Adrian's office."

"Really?" Her lips pursed. "They can do that?"

"Apparently. If you piss Sister Constance off enough."

"I told you to take the journals more seriously."

I blew out a puff of annoyed air. "It's whatever."

She shot me a sly grin, which I only saw briefly as I tugged my jersey over my head. "Sooo, is he as hot up close?"

I pulled my fluffy hair out of my shirt and up into a messy ponytail. "Even hotter, if you can believe it."

She clicked her tongue. "What a waste."

Without segue, she grabbed my arm and dug her fingers into the tender flesh of my bicep. "Halloween weekend. There's going to be a party at Brett Coleman's house. Are you coming?"

"Doesn't he live out in the middle of nowhere?"

Saint Agnes was located in Oxcreek, Kentucky, a sprawling town nestled on the southern edge of Louisville. It was kind of a weird place to live. It had a small-town vibe with rustic antique shops, old diners, and a downtown hub located on an aptly named Main Street, but there were large subdivisions, large houses on larger land plots, and, obviously, money. Hence the huge Catholic high school. You didn't have to live in Oxcreek to attend SAHS, which accounted for some students living further out, like Brett, whose CEO dad used to drop him off at school in a sleek Benz before he got his license.

"It's a barn party."

Oh, yay. Nature. "Do you have a costume yet?"

"I'm slutty Marie Antoinette."

I laughed. "Nice." I would just use my old stand-by, slutty schoolgirl, because I wasn't the kind of person who already had my outfit for an October event planned in August.

She turned her back to me, ponytail swinging. It was an unspoken ritual. We had both learned to braid from the older girls during a summer soccer camp, but Bridget's were sloppy, and my technique was crisp. I made quick work of the silky blonde strands and flipped it back over her shoulder.

The locker room started to empty, and we followed the rest of the team out onto the field.

"Academy plays hard," she said, "so don't be afraid to rough them up."

"Aye, aye, Captain."

TWO

SINCE WE HAD LIVED in the same house for so long, my room was like a time capsule, persevering the varying interests and obsession of middle school through early high school Sophia. I was too lazy to redecorate the whole thing for every phase I was in, so I just kept adding new stuff over old stuff. The walls were robin's egg blue (yuck) and covered in almost every school medal and certificate I'd ever won; twinkle lights hung as a headboard; glow-in-the-dark stars dotted the ceiling; Evanescence and boy band posters overlapped Mia Hamm and *Lord of the Rings* promos. My mom had inexplicably let me paint my own furniture, so I had a purple dresser and a garish lime green desk, both covered in flowers from my floral phase.

I sat at my desk, art supplies and scraps of paper scattered everywhere, working on a couple weeks' worth of

Art III homework. Mrs. Pearson was fortunately very tolerant of the ebb and flow of our creative muses, especially for her higher-level classes. Which was a good thing for me. My muse tended to be a finicky bitch, which didn't mesh well with the fact that I was also a huge procrastinator. I worked better under pressure anyway.

Our assignment was to reinterpret a famous piece of art. I had chosen to work with *The Creation of Adam* from the Sistine Chapel ceiling. Mrs. Pearson loved Michelangelo, so I was also hoping to score some bonus points.

I chewed on an eraser. I had turned the near-touching hands of God and Adam into Adam and Eve, with a fat apple in the middle encircled by grasping fingers. Eve's were long and delicate; Adam's thick and coarse. I was working on getting the shine just right on the apple. I smudged the colored pencil with a knuckle.

There was a rap on the door, and my mom shouted, "Turn it down in there!"

I started and almost sent colored pencils skittering. I knocked the power button on my radio with a toe. "Mom!" I swiveled to face her. "You scared the shit out of me."

"Watch your language."

No matter what I had going on after school, I still usually beat my mom home by several hours every night, so I was used to having the place to myself.

She was still in her work clothes: sensible blouse, slacks, and heels. "I brought dinner," she said.

Most nights, I was on my own for dinner, except for the occasions where I would cook for us or Mom would bring take out. My cooking skills were limited to boxes and cans, so I think Mom preferred the takeout.

"Yum. What did you bring?"

"Pizza."

"Pineapple?"

She smiled. "Of course, sweet girl." She walked farther into the room, eyeing my sketchbook. "What are you working on?"

I looked back down at the drawing. I still had lots to do, and it needed a background. Mrs. Pearson always yelled at me for skipping the backgrounds. "Homework."

"Mhmm." She rubbed the top of my head. "Sophia." I felt a tug on my messy bun, and then she held a white colored pencil out in front of my face.

"Ah-ha! I've looking for that sucker."

She shook her head as she handed the pencil to me. "Do you have a game tomorrow?" I nodded. We'd have at least two games a week for the foreseeable future. "Can you get me a schedule? I want to try to make some of your home games."

"Don't worry about it, Mom."

A line appeared between her brows as she frowned down at me. It really was okay, but I don't think she believed me, though I had been trying to convince her for years. I was well aware that we only had the things we did because my mom busted her ass at work. I wasn't going to add to her plate by being some dipshit kid who whined about their mom missing games. There were plenty of other parents there who'd cheer for me.

"Still. Make sure you get me your schedule. I'll give it to Amy, and she can see about getting me out of the office a little earlier." She continued to stroke my head.

"Thanks, Momma."

"Come eat and tell me about school."

I grimaced to myself. My mom was pretty lenient, but I wasn't sure even she would approve of my two new crushes: the boy and the man.

ele

We won that game and then the next few games, and Bridget ended up on the front page of the sports section of the newspaper...again. Sister Constance cut it out of the paper and taped it to one of the gray filing cabinets at the front of the classroom.

It really was a beautiful moment. Bridget was bringing a stray ball down from the air. Her left leg was fully extended to catch it while she balanced on the toe of her right foot. Her ponytail and left arm were parallel to the ground, and you could clearly see the muscle definition in her thighs, even in black and white and shades of gray.

Bridge was immensely pleased with herself and joked about signing autographs if anyone wanted one. I only had to put up with her during Devotional Studies, but I found any excuse to escape class that week. I'd ask ridiculous questions, continue to answer journal prompts with inappropriate pictures, and just be a general nuisance so Sister Constance would quickly lose her patience with me.

On Thursday, when I pointed out that patience was a virtue, she chucked an eraser at my head and told me to go find Mr. Ballon. Mr. Ballon was the assistant football coach, and he was in charge of detention, which tended to fill with football players and turn into an impromptu strategy session.

Ironically, I couldn't find detention and ended up in Father Adrian's office instead...but only after I had detoured to the bathroom to throw on some eyeliner.

He was seated on the edge of the big mahogany desk, waiting for me.

"Sophia," he said in greeting. I loved the way his lips curved around my name. Sophia...Sophia...Sophia... Sophia...

I took my customary chair and rummaged around in my backpack. "I brought you something." I pulled out a piece of sketch paper and handed it to him.

Mrs. Pearson had already seen my take on *The Creation of Adam*, which I had titled *Eve's Apple*, so I had spent a ridiculous amount of time removing it from my sketchbook and meticulously tearing off the little paper tag things.

His brow wrinkled as he scrutinized my drawing. My leg was bouncing, and I felt short of breath as if I'd just finished running. I never put my serious work up for public examination. It was mine. Personal. Secret. Art said something about the soul of the artist. An artist and her work were intrinsically linked. What if he didn't like it? I'd be crushed. I don't think I could handle it. A basic homework assignment seemed like a safer option.

"Beautiful."

"What?" We were so close, I had trouble concentrating. His leg was barely six inches from my own. But the white square of his clerical collar at the base of his throat—so stark against the black—was a blazing barrier. A reminder of who, what, he was.

"Your drawing. You have a gift, Sophia." When he stared at me like that, I could see the incredible blue of his eyes. A dark blue wrapped around the softer blue of his irises.

I found a small statuette of Jesus to look at instead. "It's just a picture," I mumbled.

He laughed. My heart thrilled at the sound. "No, it is much more than that. You have an ability to capture the subtle beauty of God's creations with a pencil and a piece of paper. Not everybody can do what you do."

I squirmed in my chair. The admiration in his voice was making me uncomfortable.

I started picking at the clear polish on my fingernails. "I could probably do better. That one was kinda rushed." Lies.

He smiled. "If this is rushed, I'd hate to see what you could come up with if you took your time."

He made to hand the drawing back to me, but I refused to take it. "Keep it."

"I was hoping you'd say that. I'll sell it when you become famous. That'll be my retirement plan." He glanced at his watch. "Aren't you supposed to be in class?"

"Only Devotional Studies."

"Well, since it's *only* Devotional Studies, feel free to stay as long as you like."

He moved back around to his side of the desk, and I had to refrain from sighing in happiness as I pulled my legs up into the big leather chair, sketchbook on my knees.

Father Adrian started scribbling in a black notebook.

I don't know what priests did all day, but he was always writing in that notebook. The silence was companionable, filled with the scratching of pencils.

THREE

October 2005

IT WAS A BALMY evening for the end of October, which was the perfect weather to dress in the least amount of clothes possible without having to wear a coat or worry about getting frostbite in inappropriate places. My mother had said as much when I appeared in the kitchen wearing nothing but a uniform skirt, a white oxford polo that I'd grown out of two cup sizes ago, and a pair of sequined flats. I grabbed a handful of Halloween candy from a bowl on the counter.

"That's for trick-or-treaters."

"Trick-or-treat."

She was rinsing dishes before putting them methodically in the dishwasher. I was banned from loading the dishwasher because I couldn't do it right. Okay, I might have deliberately done the dishes horrendously wrong one time because dishes were my most hated chore. I felt the rinsing was a tad redundant, but then again, this was the woman who rinsed paper plates before throwing them away.

"I'm glad to know all the money I spend on uniforms goes to good use. The black bra is a nice touch."

"I thought so."

"Where are you going?"

"Some kid's house out in the country."

"Who's driving?"

"Bridget."

"How late?"

"Don't wait up." No matter how banal the party was, we would be some of the last to leave.

"That's comforting."

"Love you." I flashed a big, toothy grin.

She finished the dishwasher and began drying her hands with the damp hand towel. She looked tired, and I had a feeling that single-parenthood was wearing on her. She was staring at a point behind my shoulder, and I felt a talk coming on. My mother had a ready-made speech for every topic: drugs, alcohol, sex, grades, boys, procrastination, teenage pregnancy, puberty. She was a small woman, slight, shorter than me, and amicable on most days, but Jesus save you if you got on the wrong side of one of her speeches. I had heard almost all of them by now and almost peed myself every time.

She folded the towel neatly and laid it out by the sink. She came around the bar counter and hugged me, and kissed my forehead. "Love you, too. Make good choices."

I wrapped my arms around her. "Always do."

Bridget arrived exactly when she said she would. Punctual as always. She looked fabulous. The real Marie Antoinette would've been jealous. Bridget even had on a powdered wig—complete with a boat—and a beauty mole. The short tulle-filled skirt of her costume would have caused quite a scandal in 18th century France. I felt frumpy in comparison.

We were on our way to the outskirts of Oxcreek, at least a forty-five-minute drive, in her glossy Mustang. The farther out we drove, the more deserted and desolate the roads became until we were on nothing more than a lane and a half, the wilderness so tight it felt like driving through a tunnel. The road was the kind of road where you expected your tires to blow out, and then you'd have to wander around in the dark to find help, only to be ultimately eaten by cannibalistic hillbillies.

I expressed this sentiment to Bridget, who rolled her eyes and adjusted the volume on the radio. Eventually, we pulled into a dirt driveway and drove straight past a large farmhouse. "Wait." I thumbed in the house's direction, which was rapidly disappearing from view. The driveway sloped gently downwards, and then I saw it: a barn. Lit up like the Fourth of July and surrounded by the haphazardly parked cars of our peers. "Are you serious?"

"Keywords, Soph. Barn. Party." She killed the engine and stuck her keys and phone in her cleavage.

"Yeah, but I thought we were all going to get belligerently drunk and maybe make farm animal noises. I wasn't expecting to actually be in a barn."

"They're the best place. Come on."

We got out of the car, and she hooked her arm through mine, giddy. I felt the music reverberating in my chest as we approached the entrance. Two thick, pretty, dumb boys were guarding the doorway.

"Ladies," said one, with a heavy twang. "A pleasure to see you."

"The pleasure's ours, Cole," purred Bridget.

Grinning, Cole handed us plastic cups. "One cup, no exceptions. Don't lose it, don't drop it."

The press of bodies as we entered was overwhelming. So was the stench. It smelled like...well, like a barn. A bouquet of wet hay, horse, and shit. Bridget and I were pushed apart almost immediately. She said something, but I couldn't hear her over the ruckus. I shrugged and smiled, waving her on. She'd be okay.

I shouldered my way out of the designated grinding area and to the outer walls. I would need significantly more alcohol before finding the courage to dive into the writhing mass of my peers. Instead, I found a dilapidated couch of unidentifiable color that didn't appear too sanitary, but it was blissfully unoccupied. Sitting on the end, I folded my legs underneath me and stared dolefully into my empty cup. It was best not to make any semblance of eye contact, but I was joined on the couch moments later anyway. He flopped down lazily, throwing an arm over the back of the couch behind my head.

"Rafael."

"What's up, Squirt?"

I gritted my teeth. "Bridget's over there." I could see her ridiculous wig bouncing merrily above the crowd.

"I saw her."

Rafael was wearing a black graduation robe with a cardboard, obviously homemade, cross hanging around his neck. There was an abnormally large protuberance tenting the front of his robe.

"Um...can I help you?" I scooted away as subtly as possible.

He laughed, smacking the thing–whatever the hell he had in his pants. "I'm a horny priest."

"Your capacity for creativity is endless."

Rafael grinned and leaned closer to me. So close, his alcohol-infused breath danced over my face. I recoiled.

"Hey." He put his free hand on my exposed knee and squeezed. "Why don't you take care of it for me?" His hand slid up my leg.

I met his glassy eyes. Then I smashed my cup into his face. He howled, and I stuck a hard elbow into his ribs for good measure. Pushing his cursing body away from me, I got up and stormed to the back entrance, which was wide open and unguarded.

I leaned against the doorframe and fumed. I knew it. I always knew Rafael was a slimy ass-wipe.

"Hey."

"What?" I snapped before I could register who had joined me.

"Is Esparza bothering you?" Boy, definitely boy. And a most surprising boy: London Hart.

I flushed the tiniest bit, trying not to think about all the time I've spent over the last two months staring wistfully at the back of his uniform khakis. "Nothing I can't handle."

"You're Sophia Salvatore, right? Number eighteen. I saw your game last week. Impressive. The way you tackled that player from Presentation, I thought she was going to punch you." He laughed.

I giggled in what I hoped was an endearing way. "Yeah, thanks." London was so adorable with his big blue eyes and expertly coifed blonde hair. He was just wearing jeans and a T-shirt. "So, what are you supposed to be?"

"Slutty schoolboy. You?"

"No way! Me too. Except I'm a girl."

He grinned. "Do you want a drink?"

"No. Lost my cup."

"Did you come here with anyone?"

"Just Bridget. Bridget James."

"Number nineteen. I know."

Of course, he knew. Everybody did. If the next words out of his mouth were "Can you introduce me" or any derivative thereof, I probably would have to smash his cup into his face.

"Do you wanna go somewhere else?"

It felt like a trick question. We were smack-dab in the middle of nowhere. Where else could we go? I glanced back into the crowd and could still see Bridget's wig bobbing over the heads of the student body. I chewed the inside of my cheek; London waited patiently, a small smile hovering.

This was what I wanted, right? It almost seemed too easy. What kind of girl would he want? Vapid Barbie girl with no opinions? I should have done more reconnaissance to beef up my "Get Boyfriend" plan instead of just leaving it as a scribble in my sketchbook.

I shrugged my shoulders, indifferent. Let him interpret that as he desired.

London set his cup on the ground and grabbed my hand, pulling me into the darkness.

———*ele*———

Somewhere else turned out to be the woods about a hundred yards from the barn. I gazed up at the blockade of trees in front of us, their spindly branches reaching into the sky like gnarled fingers.

"Are you a serial murderer?" I didn't think anyone saw us leave.

He still held my hand. "No. Do you trust me?"

"No."

"Come on." London was grinning. "Race ya." He threw himself into the trees, making about the same amount of noise as a small elephant might.

"London!" I yelled. "I'm in delicate footwear!" There was no reply. Wringing my hands, I followed London's path.

By the time I found the lake, London had already discarded his shoes, rolled up his pants, and splashed out into the water until it hit the bottom of his makeshift cuffs.

He motioned for me to join him. When I shook my head, he put his hands on his hips and pouted. "Get in the water."

"No."

"Stop being a snob. Get in the water."

"I am not a snob." I resisted the strong urge to stomp my foot. "I just don't know anything about you."

"What's your favorite color?"

"Green."

"Mine's yellow. Get in the water."

I tugged on my skirt, palms sweaty. His infallible logic was hard to argue with. I abandoned my own shoes and plunged into the warm water.

"That's better."

"Not really." I was stepping on unidentified objects, and who knew how many drunks had pissed in the lake.

London leaned over, trailing his fingertips over the top of the water, looking like trouble in his white shirt. He suddenly charged me, moving through the water with more speed than I thought possible, and seized me around the waist. I squealed appropriately before he lifted me bodily through the air and dunked me.

I surfaced, gasping but trying not to get any water in my mouth. "You jerk! Do you know how long it takes to make my hair look like this?"

"Yes."

I lunged at him, but he evaded my grasp. We continued to yell and splash around until I'd had my revenge, and London was so soaked, he had to hold his pants up. He walked back to the bank and collapsed with a huff on the muddy shore. I wandered a little farther out, the murky lake bottom sucking at my bare feet. Gross. We were well and truly in the middle of nowhere. The dark water slipped away into the distance, farther and farther away from the flickering lights of the barn.

"Sophia." I turned around. London was upright, his elbows propped on his knees. He extended a hand. "Come here."

I took his hand when I reached the bank and sat down beside him. I wiggled my toes in the cool mud. We stared at the still water. I racked my brain for something to say, but he beat me to it.

"It's your turn. To ask a question."

"Oh. What are your parents' names?"

"Bob and Jean."

I snorted. "Seriously?"

"Seriously."

"And you got London?" I would bet money it was one of those where-you-were-conceived names.

"Uh-huh. That's two questions, rule-breaker. My turn. What do your parents do?"

"These questions are pretty tame." I pulled my knees up and wrapped my arms around my legs. Now wet, the chill air raised the hair of my arms. At least, I thought it was the air. It could also have been the proximity of London's body to mine.

"We'll get to the sordid stuff later."

"My mom works at Keating and Davis Law—"

"She's a lawyer?"

"Uh, yeah." People always heard lawyer and immediately thought of dramatic courtroom scenes and slimy bad guys, ala *Law and Order: SVU*. In reality, it was a lot of long nights and paperwork. "My dad, um, left. When I was little."

There was a long pause.

He squeezed my hand gently. "I'm sorry. I didn't mean to bring that up. If you wanna go..."

"No. It's fine. I don't even remember much."

It was a standard reply I had spent years perfecting. How was I supposed to tell this random boy—practically a stranger—that my dad had already checked out long before he left us? That I didn't even hear from him save for two cards per year, one for my birthday and one for Christmas? The first few were stamped with the return address of a rehab facility four states away; the rest came from a residential address in another city. He never wrote anything in the cards except *Love, Dad*. It didn't even look like his handwriting.

London had the most devastated look on his face—like I'd just kicked a puppy. Had I been too flippant? "I'm fine, really. It's my turn. Why did you talk to me tonight?"

He looked out over the water, smiling to himself. The tension had fizzled out. "'Cause you're cute when you kick ass."

I smiled too as we lapsed into silence, and I couldn't tell if it was awkward or not.

Suddenly, he leaned over, and I froze, heart racing. Was he going to kiss me? So soon?? Was that supposed to happen right now while I was sopping, hair stringy and crunchy from wet hairspray, mascara running?

His forearm brushed across the tops of my boobs, and I jerked back. He laughed but kept coming. He picked a wad of mud and moss off my shoulder and held it up, brows raised.

"Oh...sorry." Great. Smooth move, Sophia. Now he thinks you think he's a perv.

He flicked the wad away and resumed his seat. The good news was that he didn't bother putting any extra space between us. We were still touching at shoulders, hips, and elbows. Okay, so maybe I hadn't ruined the whole thing after all.

"Yeah, so, this was fun," I said.

God, no wonder I'd never had a boyfriend.

It was a good thing London turned out not to be a deranged serial killer because I needed him to drive me home. After our romp in the mud, we trudged back up to Coleman's barn to find the rest of our peers thoroughly wasted and Bridget and Rafael conspicuously missing. She was not answering her phone, so London, being the chivalrous gentleman that he was, offered me a ride. He drove a modest—no extended cab—gray and black truck with a red pinstripe. It was cute. He even had a tarp so I didn't spoil the interior.

Bridget called the next day, apologizing profusely for abandoning me at the party.

We had a two-hour-long phone session discussing who ditched who and dissecting the events of the night. That meant I had to spill the beans about London. Bridget was ecstatic and wanted to know every saucy detail; I had to assure her that nothing earth-shattering occurred. She promised me we would make it happen. While I wasn't completely positive what "it" was, I was sure that I didn't want Bridget anywhere near it.

On Monday, I was walking to first period with Emma Reardon, the fourth member of our friendship quartet, when someone—it was Bridget—grabbed my arm and diverted my course towards the sophomore hall bathroom. The room had a damp basement smell, and the walls were stippled in blue-gray concrete. Half-moon circles had been carved out of the stall doors (because that was supposed to deter us from doing something?), the paint was chipping, and only some of the latches worked. Needless to say, we were not in the classiest bathroom in school. Therefore, it was the perfect place for smoking and other covert activities.

Bridget dragged me into the largest stall. I smiled and waved at Noreen Blue, who was leaning up against the sink playing with her hair, her eyes lined in a ridiculous amount of heavy black eyeliner—in direct violation of Section 8, Article 1 of our Code of Conduct. Her gaze darted down to our interlocked fingers and back up again. She raised her thin eyebrows. No wonder it had taken eleven years for a boy to notice me; everyone thought Bridget and I were an item. Although this notion never seemed to have an adverse effect on Bridget's social life.

She sat me down on the toilet—I tugged my skirt down to protect my legs from the seat—and bolted the door.

"Rafael and I are back together."

And this information needed to be imparted in the secrecy of the bathroom? I barely contained my grimace. Now was probably the appropriate time to let her know what a sleaze he was. "When'd that happen?"

"Over the weekend."

"Do you think that's the best idea?"

"We're going to take it slow."

"Bridge, I—"

She flapped her hands in my direction. "I don't wanna talk about him anymore. Let's talk about London." Cue impish grin.

I couldn't help but let her excitement over the whole affair infect me a little as well. I shrugged. "What's left to talk about? I told you everything already." He didn't ask for my phone number. I wouldn't see him again until Earth Science, and then I would have to contend with the curious gazes of all my classmates—including Rafael—if I attempted to...what, flirt, with him? UGH.

She frowned. "You're no fun. Whatever. Just as long as it doesn't interfere with your game today."

"I doubt it."

There was sudden banging on our door. We both jumped.

"Bridget, Sophia, are you in there?"

Bridget jerked the door open. "Shit. Shelby."

Shelby was tiny and precious, her dark hair pulled back in a slick ponytail, face split in a wide grin. "Y'all havin' a party in here?"

"Nope. I'm being a party pooper," I said.

"Oh, you're funny."

"I know. That's why you keep me around. For my witty banter."

Bridget snorted.

Shelby laughed. "So, Soph," she said, hanging off the door frame. "Did you do the assignment Ruther gave us?"

I did. That morning while I ate my Cheerios. Every night, Mrs. Ruther would make us outline sections of our history textbook. Every. Single. Night. She did give the athletes two free homework passes, though, which made the monotonous homework tolerable. But I had already used mine. Apparently, Shelby had too.

I pulled the outline out of my backpack and gave it to her.

JESSICA MINYARD

"You're amazing." She disappeared.

"I hate that fucking class." Bridget grabbed my arm. "Let's go before we start to stink."

Game day fever was in the air. The nervous, jittery energy infected all of us—me, Bridget, and Shelby—and it was all we could talk about. Of course, this wasn't just any game. It was the first game in the district tournament against a team we'd already played and who'd been leading by one point the entire game, until the last seven minutes. Emma wasn't on the team, so she tended to zone out or do homework during these heated discussions.

Kensie Walston, our keeper, had a breakdown during lunch while Bridget and Shelby were discussing strategy. She was reduced to a hiccuping, sobbing mass of seventeen-year-old girl. It took many hugs and heartening words to stop the hyperventilating.

I shouldn't have even worried about Earth Science because none of the football players were in attendance. Where the hell did they all go? I tried not to look too disappointed as I took my seat in the back row next to Rafael, who had earbuds in and didn't even look at me. Jerk.

By the time we made it alive to the locker rooms, you could cut the tension with a knife—and not even a particularly sharp one. And the game wasn't even until

42

5:30. The team dispersed to kill time until kickoff with Bridget's inspiring words ringing in their ears: if you touch a cookie, glass of milk, hamburger, etc. I'm gonna make you run laps until you puke it back up. Girls went home, went to hang out at Subway, or went to the gym to watch the basketball team practice. I stayed in the locker room with Shelby and did homework. I successfully finished embellishing a portrait of George Washington in my textbook.

We were all dressed, making minor adjustments to hair and jerseys, and ready to go on the field at five. The other team was there in their dark maroon uniforms, bouncing like raisins across the grass.

We had a pretty sizeable crowd; the bleachers were filling quickly. One section was occupied by the football team in a rare show of support and solidarity. They were being led in a chant, spelling out "Go Saint Aggies," but it ended up being more like "Go Sant Aggs." I searched for London's gold head in the crowd; he waved. I waved back, a stupid grin plastered all over my face.

Bridget had us warm up by taking a half-lap and then a short passing drill. We gathered on our end of the field in a lopsided circle to stretch. I was bent over, ass up, legs spread, palms flat on the ground, viewing the world from upside down and between my legs, when I saw him. Father

Adrian was working the crowd—pretty as you please—shaking hands with parents. Like a rock star.

My stomach dropped up into my throat, and I choked a little bit. We continued stretching, me trying to keep an eye on Father Adrian through my contorting limbs.

We were summoned to the bench by our coach, Joely, who taught Freshman English. She was new to Saint Agnes and the girls' varsity team when we were freshmen. She was young, probably early twenties, but who could really tell with teachers. I remembered she caused quite the stir her first year because she was so pretty, with shiny platinum hair and the sculpted body of an athlete. The stupid boys in her classes were ridiculous and even more immature than usual.

"Gather round." She sat down on the bench while we jostled each other to get close enough to see the dry-erase board propped on her knees. The board was green and had white lines demarcating the field lines. There were eleven Xs scribbled on, each with a name underneath. We were playing a four-four-two formation. Two strikers (Bridget and I), two midfielders and two wings, and four on defense (a right and left fullback, a stopper, and sweeper). And then pale-faced Kensie in goal.

Bridge won the coin-flip, and then it was all downhill from there. At least for me. I could not hold my side of the field. I ran myself ragged ball-chasing and consistently losing a hard-won ball to the enemy. Not only could I not hold onto a ball, but the balls I won, I could do nothing with. Passes fell short, shots swerved wide, the ball bounced erratically off my toe, instep, shin guards. It was a royal debacle, and the sloppier my touches became, the more frustrated I grew, leading only to more careless moves.

During a brief lull in the action, Bridget yelled, "Put it away!"

She was referring to whatever I was carrying around in my head that made me play like shit. A coach I had in middle school when we still played on rec leagues for fun used to say that there was a filing cabinet in our minds and that everything that didn't have anything to do with soccer needed to be stuffed in a drawer and hidden away until the game was over.

Only I couldn't put away, file, or otherwise disperse of it. It was sitting on the sidelines, just outside of my peripheral, sticking out like a sore thumb.

The end came quickly.

Play was occurring on our end of the pitch; a fierce battle was taking place between our defense and their leading striker. I took this opportunity to sneak a glance toward the crowd. I spent too much time searching for Father

Adrian's face. A black and white missile came hurtling through the air—I turned my head just in time—and crashed landed into my face.

I doubled over, clutching my face. It was on fire, metaphorically, making my eyes sting. There was no crying in soccer, so I bit down any would-be tears and contented myself with cussing rather loud and unimaginatively. "Shitmotherbitchfuckdamn."

I tasted the blood in my throat first before it began to gush out my nose. The whistle blew. Hands on my shoulders guided me over to the bench.

"Are you okay?" Joely asked.

"Yeah, I'm fine." My voice was muffled by my hands and the increasing blood flow from my nose.

"Come here." She pushed me over to the nearest trash can so I could drip into the refuse. "Milton, you're in."

Tasia Milton leaped gleefully to her feet, anxious to take my place.

"I'm fine, really." Drip, drip, drip.

Joely had a handful of medical gauze, which she pressed over my nose. She felt up my face with white-tipped fingernails. "Is that tender?"

"Owwwwww."

"It's not broken, but you'll probably bruise." She tugged at my jersey. "Give me that before you get blood on it."

I pressed the gauze tight to my face and let her pull the jersey over my head, trying to keep my bloody hands off the pristine white fabric. Blood was infinitely harder to wash off than grass stains; besides, the refs still let you play with grass stains. Blood, not so much.

Joely tossed my beautiful number eighteen on a pile of sports bags and returned to her vigil on the touchline; the tender ministrations were over. Someone, Sarah McIntosh —or Team Mom, as some affectionately called her— handed me another gauze pad and a water bottle. Mt. Vesuvius had slowed to a mere trickle; I tossed the used gauze into the trash to rest atop the remains of Gatorade bottles, candy wrappers, and old Band-Aids. Instead of taking a seat on the wooden bench with the rest of the team, I took up residence all by my lonesome on a set of metal bleachers on the track.

It was only moments before London came jogging up with a handful of those nasty brown paper towels you find in public restrooms, the kind that feel like you're rubbing sandpaper across your skin. He proffered the towels to me. "I thought you might need these."

London was so thoughtful. Here I was, half-naked (glad I'd worn the nice tank top), hair in wild disarray, bleeding, sweaty, probably smelly, and he came to my rescue with paper towels. I sat up straighter so my squishy bits wouldn't be quite so noticeable. "Thanks."

I took half, and he kept half, getting them damp with the water bottle. London helped me clean the blood off my hands and face—especially the creases of my nose. He got up and threw away the soiled towels. The pain in my face had receded to a dull throb. I poked my cheeks gingerly.

London resumed his seat next to me, our shoulders touching. "That's going to leave a mark."

"Yeah."

We sat and watched the time tick away from the first half, the score frozen at 0-0.

"Penny for your thoughts."

I smiled. "Girl problems."

He nodded as if that explained it all. I supposed somehow it did, but no boy ever ventured further into the realm of "girl problems."

"I'll be working at DQ tomorrow night if you wanna stop by. I can get you free ice cream."

"How'd you know I couldn't resist free ice cream?"

"Lucky guess. So I'll see you there?"

"Sure."

He got up just as the buzzer on the scoreboard went off, and the center ref gave two short blasts on his whistle. I jumped to my feet and quickly joined the huddle of my teammates, crowding around for water.

"Ladies, ladies." Joely clapped her hands to gain our attention. "Their defense is strong, so we're going to have to step up our offense." Several heads turned surreptitiously in my direction. "Christie, I want you to take a more offensive position. Support Bridget and Tasia. We'll start how we came off."

The refs signaled the end of halftime., and I elbowed my way to Joely. "Coach! Coach, I'm ready to go back in."

She barely glanced in my direction. "We'll see. Take a break."

The teams were taking up their assigned spots on the field. If I didn't go in now, it would be too late; I would have to wait for the next stop in play to be substituted. "But I've been taking a break. I'm ready."

"Sit down, Sophia. Let other people play."

The second half had begun. I collapsed on the bench, flabbergasted. Let other people play? Were we suddenly a U-6 team where everyone got equal playing time? Joely never seemed to care about that when she ran me a full varsity game and then a full JV game. I started playing JV for St. Aggies in the seventh grade. I had made the All-District Team and All Girls Sub-Sectionals last season. I had one bad day, and suddenly my spot was usurped by a sophomore who hadn't dedicated five years to this team? Attending soccer camp after soccer camp and starting conditioning in May to prepare for the upcoming season? Who hadn't been playing this sport since she was four years old and broken one arm, three toes, and sprained an ankle in the process? I knew life wasn't fair, but this was absurd. Not to mention humiliating and degrading.

Shelby, sweat rolling down the sides of her face, elbowed me in the ribs. "Stop being so dramatic."

"I'm not being dramatic."

"Yes, you are. I can see it in your face."

A game as viewed from the bench was an excruciating experience. I could only watch, helpless, as events unfolded. I could scream and holler like everyone else, but that was ineffective at the best of times. So, I sat and pouted, repeating every play in my head as it would have happened if I was out there.

Joely made a couple of substitutions, mostly for wing and defensive players, and Bridget came out once for water. She took a quick gulp, tossed the paper cup on the ground, and was back at the center line.

We lost 1-0.

After the customary end-of-game revelry—I missed the days when we used to get treats and juice boxes—which included the handshake (good game, good game, blah blah

blah), the team started gathering up their things. I stripped off my gear, stuffed it all in my bag, and slung the bag across my back. No one said a lot to me. There was a general mutter of trite conversation, anything but talking about the game and trying to avoid listening to the noises of joy coming from the other bench.

Bridget huffed past me, throwing, "I told you not to let that boy get to you," over her shoulder.

I could feel heat rush through my body. She was going to lecture me about boys?

"Hey." Heads turned our way. "Y'all lost that game without me." It was my turn to huff past Bridget's pink-cheeked face.

I lost myself in the sweep of the crowd heading for the parking lot or concession stand for last-minute snacks. Happy banter surged around me. After all, they'd gotten a good show—what did it matter? The game was quickly fading to the backs of their minds, replaced by other trivial concerns about life. They hadn't been benched. Or had a tiny ball of white-hot, pissed-off anger steadily growing inside their chests.

I pushed my way to my car, a tiny two-door silver Honda, popped the trunk and tossed my shit inside. I shut it with more force than completely necessary. There were still people on the field, eerily fluorescent green under the harsh stadium lights. Kids were running around with wild abandon, moms had stopped to chitchat, random girls and football boys had merged together for a flirty game of let's-kick-the-ball-as-hard-as-possible-toward-the-net.

I got in my car and left before the parking lot could get too busy. As I pulled out onto the main highway, a figure loomed out of the darkness like some kind of holy apparition. I would recognize that ass anywhere, even on the side of the road. Drumming my fingers on the steering wheel, I slowed to a lazy trundle, watching him walk in and out of my headlights.

I jerked to the right and skidded to a crunching halt. I checked my face in the rearview mirror, but there just wasn't anything I could do about the puffy cheeks and the dark bruises already forming under my eyes. I was going to look splendid tomorrow. Unbuckling my seatbelt, I fumbled clumsily out of the car, banging my knee on the door.

"Father Adrian!" I screamed his name. Just a little.

He stopped, turned around, waved a greeting. He was wearing a flimsy, gray-green jacket over his usual dour black.

"Do you need a ride?" He took a couple of steps forward and hesitated, looking as though he'd just been caught doing something naughty. "I don't bite, I promise."

"I didn't think you did." He grinned and walked purposefully toward me and the car.

I got in, giddy as a nerd on the first day of school. "Where to, Padre?"

"The church."

Father Adrian filled the passenger side of my small car— shoulders hunched and legs squished up next to the dashboard. "You can move the seat back." He fumbled under the seat to no avail. "Here." I reached over, my forearm brushing the side of his thigh, and found the latch with sure fingers. The seat slid back with an audible click.

Father Adrian rubbed his knees with his long-fingered hands. "Thank you."

I smiled. "*Je vous en prie*. So, um, no car?"

"The parish has a car, but it's otherwise occupied."

"But you don't?"

"I took a vow of poverty."

"So, you're poor?"

He laughed. "Not exactly. I claim no possessions. So, no car."

"Oh." I was so eloquent sometimes. "Do you walk home often? In the dark?"

"Occasionally."

"Aren't you scared of getting into some kind of trouble?"

"Would you mug a priest?"

Naw, I could think of better things to do to them. I shook my head. "Not if you're poor." Cue hearty giggle.

It was a good thing the church was only ten minutes from school because I'd already run out of things to say. He smelled nice. Not the heavy musk that came from some boys who bathed in too much cologne. His scent was subtle, clean. It filled my car and was a lot harder to ignore than his physical form.

I drove into the empty church parking lot, up a steep hill, and stopped in the fire zone in front of the parish hall.

"Where do you live?"

"There is a set of apartments behind the hall." He pointed to a set of wooden stairs that wrapped around the side of the building.

"That's cool." Me and my rapier wit struck again. "Well, here we are!"

I glanced over to find him studying me with eyes that were black in the meager glow of one lonely floodlight. There was a soft patter on the windshield. His gaze flicked briefly to the raindrops.

"Just in time," he said.

He leaned across the console to tuck a few wispy strands of unruly hair behind my ear. My ear went hot as he brushed against it.

Or, my first impression was that he was tucking my hair, but his hand came away with a clump of prickly grass. "You had grass in your hair," he said.

Then he was gone, jogging to the stairs, a dark figure disappearing into the night and misty drizzle.

I was left alone with nothing but the rush of blood in my ears and the pounding of my heart.

Jesus-fucking-Christ.

FOUR

November 2005

BRIDGET DROVE AS IF Mario Andretti had been her driving instructor and other cars were just challenges on her obstacle course.

"I'd like to live," I said.

She scoffed. "If you insist."

She was in a fine mood, overly excited and in a hurry to get to my pseudo/maybe/kinda/sorta date with London Hart. Naturally, I had invited the girls. Shelby was squeezed between the front seats, playing with the radio; Emma was in the back complaining about Shelby's song choices.

Bridge and I had made up the day after the soul-crushing game at lunch. We'd then had a cathartic bitch-fest about Joely and the fact that she'd already handed out conditioning schedules for the spring and registered most of us for the indoor league. Then I told them about London's invite, which was met with many squeals of joy. Bridget had insisted I come over to her house beforehand so she could dress me.

That was a mistake.

I'll admit I was thankful for her help with the makeup; I didn't look like a clown, and she had done her best to lessen the effects of the nasty, purplish bruises that had formed under and around my eyes and across the bridge of my nose. But she had also made me squeeze my butt into the only pair of skinny jeans I owned. I could barely breathe or walk, the button digging painfully into my soft belly flesh. My thighs were very close friends—they liked to touch. I was mildly afraid I was going to set fire to myself because of the friction. Other than that, she had approved my Henley—blue-and-green stripes with a white sequined cami—a pair of gray flats, and a long, silver lariat my mom gave me on my sixteenth birthday. She'd straightened my hair, too.

We strutted into Dairy Queen as if we owned the place, confident in our unmarred youth. It was always cold and abnormally bright, no matter the season. The counter with its two cash registers was what you saw first. To the right was a set of steps that went into a shallow recession, lined on both sides with booths. The tables to the back, next to the restrooms, were always filled with toothless old men in blue jumpers chain-smoking.

Bridget led the way to a booth in our usual section, where we could see and be seen by people at the counter. There was a woman and her daughter at London's register. He was laughing and smiling freely. Emma and Shelby were both staring at me with arms crossed. Bridget was twirling her keys around on the tabletop.

"Well?" said Emma.

"He's busy," I said.

Shelby looked over her shoulder, dark ponytail swinging. "Not anymore."

It was true. The woman and her Dilly-Bar-bearing kid had moved on. Still, I sat, wringing my hands. "I don't know. He's working."

"Annnnd?" Emma pressed, dragging out the word.

"It feels weird. Bothering him at work."

Shelby scoffed. "Bothering?"

"He invited you, remember?" Bridget chimed in.

"Yeah, but –"

"Stop being a chicken," said Shelby.

"You're his girlfriend, so it doesn't matter," Emma chirped.

I made some kind of unintelligible noise of protest. "I am not his girlfriend."

"If it talks like a girlfriend, walks like a girlfriend, acts like a girlfriend, guess what? It's a girlfriend." Bridget flashed a wry smile.

"Thanks for that, Socrates," I growled.

"You are most welcome. Now, get moving. I didn't come here just to watch y'all breathe."

I got up slowly, while Shelby clapped, and meandered up to the counter with what I hoped was a "come hither" swing. But probably not, considering how tight my pants were. London was waiting with a big, stupid grin on his face, his red and navy DQ hat cocked to the side on top of his stupidly perfectly swoopy hair. "Hey."

"Hi." We were off to an excellent start.

"Your face looks better."

"You always know exactly what to say to make a girl feel good."

"One of my many talents. I see you brought company." He waved. They waved back enthusiastically. I flushed. "I was kinda hoping to have you all to myself."

The flush crept down my neck. "I was lured here on the promise of ice cream. No ice cream, no deal."

He winced. "You drive a hard bargain."

In no time, London conjured up four small cones, filled them with soft serve, and dipped them in chocolate. He gave me two and then came out from behind the counter carrying the other two and a bunch of napkins. He walked me back to my booth. "Girls," he greeted, helping me divvy out the ice cream cones. Before I could sit down, London grabbed my elbow, steering me a few feet away and safely out of earshot.

"Sophia, I do have a question for you."

"Okay."

"I was wondering if you'd maybe, sometime, when you're free...want to kind of hang out with me...at some point?"

He was even cuter when flustered.

"That has got to be the worst way to ask someone out I've ever heard." Not that I'd been asked out a lot, but still.

"Is that a yes?"

"Yeah, for sure."

"Good."

He grabbed my arm and bit off the curly top of my ice cream cone. Then he hurried back to work, and I returned to my friends, holding the cone to my chest like a treasure. Three expectant faces greeted me.

"We're officially going out."

They erupted in excited twittering. I guess it was exciting when your last chronically single friend finally got a date. I stared at the teeth marks in my chocolate coating, little butterflies fluttering around in my chest. I suddenly didn't know what to feel or what to do or what to think.

I had a date. And maybe a boyfriend. But I think we had to go on a date first. And then there was the stuff that happened after the date. I didn't have that part quite planned out yet.

It was Friday night, and Eaton's was dead. Eaton's was usually dead, but Friday nights were especially dead. We might have been a small town, but everyone could always find something better to do than hang out at the drugstore.

Except me.

I only worked a couple nights a week during the season, but those nights were hell. We're open till 10:00. It was 9:05. Mr. Eaton was shuffling around behind the pharmacy counter, and I was manning the retail register. He wouldn't dare have us close one minute early—God forbid some old lady come tottering in needing her meds—and I knew better than to ask.

I watched the arm of the clock. Tick, tick, tick.

9:06.

I sprawled over the counter with my sketchbook open and a stack of charcoal pencils at the ready. Mr. Eaton didn't mind if I worked on homework during my shift as long as I still got everything else done, which wasn't much. We had self-portraits due in my Art III class next week.

I hated self-portraits; they never turned out the way I thought they should. It was like looking at yourself in the mirror, thinking you looked damn fine, and then taking a picture. Never the same. I mean, was I really that weird-looking? Did my nose really slant at such a wonky angle?

Perhaps.

The bell above the front door tinkled, and my head snapped up with interest. But it was only Rafael Esparza and JJ Warren. Frick and frack. They both glanced my way as they sauntered through the door, and I rolled my eyes and grimaced.

They made a beeline for the refrigerated section, and I resumed my sketches.

I wasn't left unaccosted for long.

They sidled up to my register with an armful of energy drinks and a box of condoms. JJ slid the Magnums across the counter, a shit-eating grin plastered to his face.

I raised my eyebrows. "You know that's a marketing tactic, right?"

"What is?"

I gestured to the box. "They're the same size as all the others. It's just a label to make you feel better and spend more."

Raf laughed, and the tips of JJ's ears turned pink. He had at least five inches on Raf and was scarily lean. Like all bones and joints and weird hollows. I don't know how he ever took a hit on the basketball court.

"Yeah, well, what do you know?"

I smiled sweetly, grabbing the handheld scanner. "A lot." I waved the scanner at him. "And I've seen your dick."

He spluttered. "That was ten years ago! Everyone saw my dick!"

I smiled reluctantly at the memory. It wasn't quite ten years, though. At our seventh-grade dance, JJ and a bunch of other boys thought it would be uproariously funny if he whipped his dick out in front of the girls of our class. We all squealed in horror, and JJ had detention for two weeks and was banned from school social functions for the rest of middle school.

I finished scanning and bagging their merch and hit a few keys on my register. "Okay, who's paying for all this?" I held up a hand.

Rafael grabbed it. "I was hoping you'd let us skate by on my good looks."

I snorted. "You're not hot enough for that."

"So you do think I'm hot?"

"I didn't say that."

"You did."

I pursed my lips. Technically, grammatically, I had inferred he was hot. But I hadn't meant it like that.

I had known Raf since Sunday school when he still had acne and skinny legs. I had ceased seeing him as a separate physical entity beyond Bridget's boyfriend.

While I was pondering this conundrum, JJ had his freakishly bony fingers all over my sketchbook. "Some of these are really good." He sounded surprised. "Mine suck." JJ was in my Art III class, so I assumed he was having as much trouble with this assignment as I. "I like this one the best."

His fingers landed on my last sketch. Where my hair covered half my face.

Raf peeked over his shoulder. "Yeah, that one is very emo, struggling artist type."

I snapped the sketchbook closed and stowed it away in safety under the counter. I could feel the splotches of red blooming on my cheeks. "Can y'all pay so I can go home sometime tonight?"

Rafael's face was stretched in a weird grimace like he was trying not to smile at my discomfiture. He pulled some bills from his wallet and let them float down onto the counter. "I hear you've got a big game tomorrow. Try to keep your eye on the ball this time."

Asshat.

———*ell*———

It was the perfect day for a game.

For early November, the weather was still Kentucky mild —chilly enough for a long-sleeve shirt under my jersey but not so cold that breathing felt like deep-throating shards of glass. It was slightly overcast, too, so your eyes wouldn't start aching from squinting.

It was late in the season for a district game, but the hosting school had trouble securing their fields. This was America, so football was first, come Hell or high water or the End of Days. Even if they never, and I mean never, won a game.

But I didn't have time to dwell on misogyny and sports. We had a district tournament to win.

Mom gave me a quick peck on the cheek and swat on the butt. "Play hard, Soph."

I gave her a thumbs-up as I made my way over to my team, who were already gathering around the visitor's benches. Joely was looking immaculate in her matching tracksuit and impeccably coifed hair. She had her lucky necklace on—a custom-made, diamond-encrusted soccer ball. She squeezed my shoulder as I swung my bag up onto the bench. I did a quick headcount of girls.

"Where's Bridget?"

She scanned the crowd. "Haven't seen her yet. She's not with you?"

I shook my head. Bridget and I usually tried to carpool to these things, but we didn't make any plans, and my mom wanted to drive me. Bridget was entirely capable of getting herself to the game—or so I had assumed.

"Have you heard from her?"

Joely rolled our practice balls onto the field for warm-up. "She'll show."

I went through the motions of getting ready. Adjusting the Under Armour under my shorts, double-socking it, and strapping on my shin guards, tying and retying my cleats, so my toes didn't fall asleep mid-game.

I was busy making a headband out of Saint Agnes-green prewrap tape when Tasia Milton grabbed my arm. Her usually golden-brown face was splotched red and white in terror. "Where's Bridget?" she whispered as if we were in a horror movie hiding from the boogeyman.

I glanced around again, eyes peeled for a high, bouncing ponytail. Nada.

Tasia's fingers were digging in painfully. I gently pried her off. "She'll be here," I said.

She had to be. Bridget was captain; she wouldn't miss such an important game. While we made it into the tournament almost every year, we hadn't actually won in almost five.

Joely was standing on the sidelines, legs braced apart, arms crossed, a thick line etched between her brows. She glanced at her watch and then spied me playing with my shoes. "Sophia. Warm them up."

Several heads swiveled in my direction. Shelby gave me a surreptitious thumbs-up.

Since the girls were milling close by, dicking with their hair and uniforms, I didn't have to raise my voice. "All right, ladies, line it up."

Our warm-up routine was basically the same every time, with minor adjustments here and there to accommodate different drills. So it wasn't rocket science to lead. Any of the girls could do it, really.

We took a half-lap around the field to get our blood pumping and then moved into our stretching circle, me in the middle, girls' voices crashing around me. I kept my eyes peeled for Bridget, and I could tell Tasia was doing the same. No Bridget meant she'd be a starting forward for the biggest game of the season. I knew what that felt like. The bilious roll of your stomach, the jittery shake of your hands.

I kept waiting for Joely to interrupt and take over, but she never did.

Not during the anthem, not during the announcement of our starting line-up, not during my call of the coin toss.

In fact, she just kept inclining her head at me every time I looked at her for confirmation that I should, indeed, be doing this.

I knew I was going to have to be strong for Tasia. She would follow my lead, even as she stepped up to take Bridget's spot next to me on the middle circle. I'd won the coin toss and picked the better side of the field to defend, which meant they got kickoff.

The first whistle blew.

I shot forward as soon as the other team touched the ball, startling them both with such an aggressive first move, and their hesitation cost them the advantage.

Tasia took off towards their goal as I hustled the ball away from the other forward. One knock from my much wider hips bumped her off the ball, and I sped after Tasia.

We didn't convert that play into a goal, but we managed with the next one.

They scored right after with an impressive long pass.

Tasia was surprisingly intuitive to how I wanted to run the field. She let me call the plays, which was a nice change of pace compared to me having to follow Bridget.

By halftime, we were still tied at 1-1, Bridget still hadn't shown, and the other team's defense had figured me out and shut me down.

Joely had figured this out too. "Shelby, I want you to move up more. Support Tasia and Sophia. Sophia, you have to change up your plays. We need to be able to get more shots on goal. Got it?"

I nodded, chewing on the edge of my plastic water cup.

The whistle blew again, and we all hurried to our positions.

I grabbed Tasia's arm. "They're going to expect me to try to run down the middle. You take the ball to the outside, and we'll test their corners."

She wiped a sheen of sweat off her forehead with the back of her hand. "Agreed."

It was our kickoff.

We posted up.

Whistle blew.

I tapped the ball and then shot forward like I'd been doing before, except this time, I didn't have the ball.

They converged on her quickly, but Tasia had some of the fanciest footwork I'd ever seen when she was on her game—and today, she was so on.

I saw it coming before it happened.

Tasia was outmaneuvering them all. She tapped the ball a few paces in front of her and was preparing to follow it when one of their girls grabbed the back of her jersey. It was just enough force to pull Tasia down.

I stopped so hard my cleats kicked up wads of grass and headed for the girl, yelling, "You little shithead!"

The center referee was frantically blowing on his whistle, right on my heels. "Can it, eighteen, or I'll eject you too!"

He had his shiny red card out and was waving it around in the air, threatening.

I reached Tasia just as Shelby crashed into my back, arms tightening around my waist—as if she could stop me from knocking the smarmy look off that girl's face.

She had her hands up in supplication. "It was an accident."

The ref finally arrived, arm held aloft stiff as a pole, and announced, "Red card on fourteen, Weldon Heights."

I pulled Tasia to her feet and brushed the dirt and grass off the back of her uniform. "Shake it off."

She nodded, but I could tell by the vacant look in her eyes that the damage had already been done. Number fourteen's expulsion wouldn't be enough to bring Tasia back into the right headspace. There are two types of soccer players in the world: those who enjoy a physical game and those who don't. Tasia was the latter, and the physicality rattled her to her core. They had shaken her up, and she never recovered.

We lost again. The second consecutive game in a row.

It wasn't Tasia's fault; I guess you could say it was mine since I missed my last penalty shot. We had still been tied up until that point.

Leaving the field was a somber affair; I didn't hang around to chitchat. Just stripped off my gear as haphazardly as I could and made a beeline for the car, my mom hurrying along in my wake.

I propped my stinky, sweaty, pale, and pruned feet up on the dash, watching Weldon Heights fade into the background.

My mom's lip curled. "Were you born in a barn?"

"No."

I pulled my feet down and stuck them under the vents instead, which were blowing warm air.

"You don't get to be sulky. It was a great game."

"We lost. It was a *losing* game."

She huffed out a breath of air that was somewhere between a sigh and a snort.

"That was our last game of the season," I informed her as if she didn't already know.

"It was a good season, Sophia. With a winning record. You don't have to have a title to be proud of what you accomplished."

But I wanted a title. I wanted them to let us hang a banner in the gym alongside the football and basketball teams. I wanted that recognition.

I continued to sulk all the way home, and my mom, in her infinite wisdom, let me. She'd said her piece.

I threw all my gear into a pile in the corner of my bedroom and flopped facedown into my pillows.

I didn't nap. Couldn't.

My frustration grew with every minute that ticked by. And my curiosity. And sense of betrayal. Eventually, I couldn't stand it anymore and snuck out of my room to fetch the cordless phone and then tiptoed back, closing the door as gently as I could.

I punched in her number, almost hoping she wouldn't pick up.

"Hello?" Her voice sounded unusually high. Like she was trying too hard to sound nonchalant.

"Where were you?" I demanded.

There was a long pause. "I'm sorry, Soph. I wasn't feeling good."

"Are you serious? It was our district game."

"I was cramping really bad."

"It was our *district* game," I repeated, for lack of anything better to say. Bridget had never missed a game because of her period—neither of us had. Hell, I could have blood running down my leg, and I'd still show up. "Well, we lost, if you care."

"I do care."

"I needed you there. Tasia is good, but she's not you."

"What do you want me to say? I'm sorry, okay?" Now she sounded peeved as if I was the one in the wrong. As if I had skipped the most important game of the season. "Listen, I've gotta go. Mom wants me to help her with something. I'll see you later."

And then the line clicked dead.

FIVE

WHEN THE TIME CAME for our first official date—as in, London was picking me up at my house—the bruise across my face had almost completely faded. Instead, there was a big ole zit right between my eyebrows, glowing like a lighthouse beacon. I popped it in one deft stroke, dabbed on some concealer, and finished getting ready.

I was sitting on the stoop under the sharp halogen light when London pulled up. I had heard the clunky roar of his truck swerving through the neighborhood long before I saw him. He met me halfway up the driveway, looking very clean-cut in a plaid sweater and dark wash jeans.

His hands were stuffed deep into his pockets. "Hey."

"Ready!" I said brightly, moving towards the passenger side.

But London moved towards my front door. He grinned sheepishly. "I thought I might come in. Meet your mom."

I was momentarily stunned. "Um. Okay." He followed close behind me—almost pressed against my back—to the door. I knocked lightly, peeked in, and called, "Mom?" praying that she was appropriately covered and not wandering around *au natural*.

I shouldn't have worried.

"Yes," she replied from the couch, where she sat in sweats, a messy bun, and reading glasses, surrounded by piles of manila folders, moving through the stacks with a red pen.

"Mom."

London followed me inside.

He grabbed my hand as soon as my mom glanced up. His palm was small, barely bigger than mine, and hot, almost scorching. I wanted to pull away but couldn't explain why.

My mom smiled, her whole face lighting up. She stood up, smoothing pants and hair. "Hello, darling. This must be London." Her eyes flicked to me as if confirming the identification.

"Yes, ma'am."

"I'm Cecelia, Sophia's mom," she gushed.

"It's nice to meet you."

They shook hands congenially. I had the feeling that if I left them at it, they would stand there and shoot the breeze for the next fifteen minutes.

"Yeah, well, we should go," I said, gently tugging London away. "Or we'll be late."

"Be safe!" My mom waved us out the door.

Dinner and a movie. The date of futility.

London took me to a small local bar and grill that was close to the movie theater. We ordered enough chili-cheese fries to feed a small village. His foot kept knocking into mine under the table, and I couldn't decide if it was intentional.

"You keep kicking me."

He flushed and cut off midsentence to mumble an apology and then resumed complaining about his conditioning schedule. "Coach has us training four days a week!"

"Mmmhmm," I conceded around a mouthful of fry. "I mean, I still can't believe she skipped that game."

He blinked. "What?"

"Bridget. One of your players wouldn't even think about skipping, would they? Your coach would have their ass on a plate and on the bench." We'd rehashed this topic several times over the course of dinner, but I still wasn't getting the response I wanted from him. What precisely, that was, I wasn't sure. "She won't be benched. She's Joely's golden girl." I mashed a fry into my plate.

"She was sick."

"That's not a good enough excuse."

"Are we ever gonna stop talking about Bridget?"

I shrugged. I didn't want to stop talking about Bridget. Not until someone else confirmed what I was thinking about her.

"Oh!" he said, bouncing a little in his seat. "Have you heard that that new freshman English teacher may be fired soon? What do you think she did?"

"How am I supposed to know?"

"You seem to know a lot," he said, sheepish.

"That's literally the worse piece of gossip I've ever heard. Don't you have something better than that? If I'm going to date the quarterback, I better get some juicy details."

He flushed redder this time, but it was more pleased than embarrassed.

And then he proceeded to tell me in lurid detail all about one of the linebacker's nasty case of jock itch.

Not exactly what I was expecting.

We walked the short distance to the theater and joined the long line of other youths who'd also managed to get their parents' permission to be out this late.

There was a huddle of upper-class football players who winked and hooted at me and London from across the lobby. He seemed to stand taller, bolstered by the attention, while I shrank away.

"Troglodytes."

"What's a troglodyte?"

I shook my head and stepped up to the counter; London intercepted me with an arm slid around my waist.

"Two for *The Faraway Autumn*," he told the ticket lady, pulling a twenty from his wallet.

Ugh, vomit. I didn't even like rom-coms.

But I took my ticket anyway with a smile. "You didn't have to pay for me again." He'd already bought dinner.

"It's a date. Do you want any snacks?"

The chili-cheese fries sitting in my stomach said no, but my heart was saying yes. So we got a large popcorn and two large drinks.

I sipped on my Cherry Coke as we made our way to our seats, London opening doors even though he was also carrying the popcorn.

The theater was mostly empty save for a trio of middle-aged women up front. Our demographic was not lining up for *The Faraway Autumn*, that was sure.

I picked out two seats in the middle of the middle, which was my favorite spot.

London handed the popcorn to me and leaned over to whisper in my ear, "These are good seats."

"We had such limited options," I whispered back.

He guffawed like it was the funniest thing he'd ever heard; I felt like he was overindulging me.

The lights went down, and the commercials came up, and that put an end to our witty banter. We munched—well, it was mostly me munching—on the popcorn as the opening credits rolled.

London leaned towards me but was careful to keep his distance. The only thing touching were our forearms on the shared armrest. His palms he kept safe and away, spread out flat on his thighs. His fingers kept twitching like he was going to reach out and grab my hand, which I conveniently kept within easy reach, but he never did.

London got me home a good fifteen minutes before my suggested curfew time. I had expected a quick make-out session in the truck since, after all, he'd kept his hands to himself during the entire movie.

What I wasn't expecting was London getting out without a word, opening my door, and then leading the way around to the back of his truck. He put one foot on the bumper and hoisted himself effortlessly over the tailgate.

"What the hell?" I blurted before I could turn on my behavioral filters.

He just laughed and held out a hand. "Come on. I want to talk."

I let him help me over, and we clambered across the bed, over the cab, down the windshield, and settled on the hood. I maneuvered myself with care, trying not to make any of the metal pop unnecessarily.

We lay, bodies almost touching, staring up at the sky so deep black, it gleamed blue. I counted fourteen stars. And one that might have been an airplane.

"I've been thinking," he started, "about your issue with Bridget."

"I thought you didn't want to talk about her anymore?"

"Well, I've had an epiphany."

Was that where all his attention was during the movie? The reason he couldn't seem to grab my hand? He was too busy solving my best friend predicament?

"I can't wait to hear about that."

"She's just not committed as you are." He said it with such conviction, like he had just solved one of the great mysteries of the universe.

I snorted, because it was such bullshit. Bridget was captain and valedictorian and any other -ian she could get her hands on. She excelled. That's literally what she did. Commitment wasn't the issue, but hell if I knew what was.

London turned his head, familiar smile bright against a shadowed face. "It's your turn."

"For what?"

"To ask a question."

I groaned, and he retaliated by poking me in the ribs. Fine, fine. I hated this stupid game. I tried to think of something good, something that would surprise him.

"Did you know I had a huge crush on you in the fifth grade?"

He laughed, unperturbed. "I had a huge crush on you, too."

"No, you didn't."

"Yes, I did. I was going to ask you to that St. Patrick's Day dance. Remember that?"

Of course, I did. I wore a hideous ankle-length beige skirt and went with Bridget and her last boy before Rafael. "Yeah. You took Beth Henderson. Why didn't you ask me? We could have been soul mates." I grinned.

"Because you're terrifying. I think that was the day you punched one new kid."

"He was a jerk." He thought it would be hilarious to pull up Shelby's skirt. Boy learned his lesson that day.

London grabbed my hand, twining our fingers and wiggling closer until our shoulders touched. "You're still terrifying, but in a sexy, badass kinda way."

My stomach flopped, giddy and nervous and exhilarated all at the same time. The tiny, uber-girl part of me was screaming, "He thinks I'm sexy!" but the badass shut her up quick and turned into London's body.

"So. Question. Are you going to kiss me any time this century?"

And then he did.

And it wasn't what I was expecting.

Maybe I thought since London had a public track record of girlfriends and girl acquaintances that he would be good at this.

He crushed his lips to mine, and we sat like that for a few seconds before he opened his mouth and attacked me with his tongue. He didn't bother waiting for my mouth to open. Also, his grip had turned vicelike on my hand, and I'm not sure why he was holding on so hard. Maybe to keep me from escaping his horrible kiss?

I almost snort-laughed into his mouth, but thankfully, he chose that moment to pull away. I was left bemused, and I'm sure I had a stupid look on my face. I resisted the urge to reach up and wipe my mouth.

He was grinning at me.

Should I say something? I should probably say something.

"Uh, great."

His smile slipped.

"Yeah, uh, great date. Yeah, I had a great time." Great date, Sophia, you imbecile.

London pulled my crushed hand up and planted a kiss to the back of it. Great, now my hand would be slobbery too. I managed to return his enthusiastic grin.

"Is your mom waiting for you?" he asked.

I glanced back at the mostly dark house; she had left the porch light on for me. "Probably."

"Well, you better get inside, then. I have a good first impression to maintain."

He leaned over and pecked my cheek.

His second kiss was far better than the first.

I'm sure my mom heard London's truck pull up, but she wasn't waiting for me in the living room as I'd expected. I tiptoed through the house—not sure why I was tiptoeing; it wasn't like I was trying to be sneaky—putting my purse down in my room first before creeping down the hallway to her bedroom.

There was a sliver of light peeking from under the door, and I could hear the soft mumble of the TV. I thought I heard her voice over the TV, but who the hell would she be talking to at this time of night? I pushed the door open gently.

Mom was nested in a pile of pillows and blankets, eyes closed, an open book on her lap, cordless on the nightstand, and *Blind Date* on the TV. It was our favorite after-midnight reality show.

"Mom."

She jerked and patted the spot next to her, all without opening her eyes.

I scurried inside and jumped on the bed, snuggling into her side and laying my head on her lap like I used to do when I was little.

"Who were you talking to?"

"No one." Her fingertips were light brushes against my temple as she stroked through my hair. "How was your date?"

"Better than theirs."

The two blind daters were both blonde and bronzed, the dude's traps almost coming up to his ears. The girl had this sour look on her face, and the thought bubble above her head said, *All I want is food*. I could relate.

"And? Do you like him?"

"I think so. How do you know?"

She laughed. "Believe me, you'll know. When you find the one, you'll know."

"Aren't you supposed to be lecturing me about boys?"

"I'm going to go out on a limb here and trust my parenting skills. You've made it this far unscathed." She ruffled my hair. "Did you kiss?"

"Mom!"

"I heard y'all come back a half hour ago. I know you were doing something out there in my driveway."

"We might have kissed."

"And?"

"It was pretty good." It was pretty wet.

"You better make sure he's a good kisser. It's going to be a tough relationship if he doesn't know how to kiss."

"I guess we'll have to practice."

"Just not where the neighbors can see you."

I snorted out a laugh and curled in deeper under her arm. I'm pretty sure none of my friends received the same kind of advice from their moms after their first date with a boy, but my mom wasn't other moms.

Bridget had her vast collection of OPI nail polishes lined up in front of her crossed legs. The color I chose, Kinky in Helsinki, was balanced precariously on the inside of one thigh. I sprawled across her bed, my hands dangling within her reach. Her tongue stuck out of the side of her mouth in concentration. She brushed on the second coat with the precision of a master painter. I'd have to take off the polish as soon as someone at school noticed, but the art of application was still fun.

"Okay"—she dipped the brush—"tell me again, and don't leave anything out."

We'd gone over my date with London, like, five times already. How he didn't hold my hand during the movie but kissed me on the hood of his truck. My theory was he saw that move in a chick-flick, and it was supposed to be romantic. Therefore, he didn't know what else to do with himself until it was time for *the* moment.

"And there was no groping? At all?" This was said incredulously.

"Not even a little."

At one point, his hand had skimmed my ribs, perilously close to under-boob, but then his lips stopped moving, and things got awkward. It was like he couldn't move his hand and mouth at the same time.

Her smile curved softly. "Well, congratulations on your first kiss."

I guess it was my first kiss, definitely the first with tongue. The chaste cheek-pecks from middle school boys didn't count, and I supposed neither did Bridget's.

Her mom had finally acquiesced to a co-ed party, at least until midnight. Bridget had caused quite the stir when her bottle spin had landed on me, and instead of turning red and spinning again like everyone else who'd landed on a classmate of the same sex, she leaned over and pressed her closed mouth to mine. We were only thirteen, so I don't know if that could be called a kiss. She'd lingered long enough to leave behind a shine of strawberry Lip Smacker.

"Uh, thanks, I guess."

Her fingers were warm and deft as she finished my nails.

"So, are you officially his girlfriend now?"

That was an interesting question coming from the girl who had pronounced us a couple before our first date. I knew what she was doing. I recognized stalling when I saw it, especially from her. She didn't want me to ask her any more questions about why she'd missed the district game and was hoping the polish fumes and lure of mint chocolate chip ice cream and campy horror movies would make me forget. I had already forgiven her, obviously, but I had not forgotten.

"Are you going to tell me why you really skipped our game?" I gave her the courtesy of not staring directly at her but blowing on my sticky nails instead.

"I did not skip."

"Skipped, missed, absconded, whatever. You weren't there."

She was scooping the polishes back into their bag, glass clinking together gently. Her brow was furrowed, and she was watching what her hands were doing, shoulders pulled tight. She frowned, and her mouth opened slightly like she was going to say something, but the words just wouldn't come out.

I pulled myself up on my elbows and gave her my full attention. "You can tell me anything, you know. Best friends forever. It says so." I tugged on the matching necklace we both wore.

Her shoulders dropped. "I was just sick, okay? I didn't want to miss, I swear." She pulled the zipper closed forcefully.

My best friend was hiding something, and she wasn't even doing a very good job of pretending she wasn't. Only I couldn't fathom what it could be. I don't remember much, if anything, getting in the way of soccer or school. Bridget made sure of that with her meticulous notes in her planner and the vicious cutting out of anything that didn't serve her purposes. She was like a maniacal social calendar gardener. Which made me wonder: was she seeing someone else? Not that I cared much for Rafael's feelings, but that would be out of character for her.

"Are you...hanging out...with someone...on the side?"

Her face morphed into shock. "You think I'm cheating on Raf?"

"Not necessarily a boy. Like, a new friend..." I trailed off aimlessly.

"You think I'm cheating on *you*?"

It was always a fear, deep in the back of my mind, that she would finally realize that she could do better than me. That she'd realize what a weirdo I was and leave me to go hang out with people more like her. With more money, with country club memberships, with two parents, with blonde hair, with more social and academic ambition. She had almost left me once for a girl named Brooke with dishwater-brown hair and chunky highlights. Brooke breezed in and out of Saint Agnes for a semester, so she was gone before I had to dispose of her.

The look on my face had Bridget laughing. She leaned up and squished my face between her hands. "You are my forever. Now, are we watching *The Ring* or *House on Haunted Hill*, Vincent Price version, not Geoffrey Rush version."

"Vincent Price, duh."

I hopped off her bed and made my way to the TV console cabinet to fetch the movie.

"Great, I'll be back with snacks!" she said gleefully and exited the room. Both our mothers were the kind of mothers who did not regularly stock what they called "junk food" but would run to the store and grab the goods when they knew we were having sleepovers. Which tended to happen a lot at Bridget's house, so Mrs. James usually kept a few things in the pantry for us.

Bridget made good on her promise and returned with a 2-liter of Vanilla Coke, a bag of chips, and a paper towel full of Oreos. I could not eat Oreos without any milk, but that did not deter Bridget; dry Oreos were her favorite sweet.

We snuggled under Bridget's floral comforter with the snack hoard cradled between us. Bridget's house was the best for hanging out because her room was upstairs and had its own TV. The lights were out, so the only illumination came from rows of twinkle lights strung on the wall behind the bed. It was the perfect ambiance for our horror movie binges.

About twenty minutes into the movie, the comforter buzzed, and I choked on a mouthful of Vanilla Coke. "Shit balls."

"Oh, relax." Bridget slid her phone out from the pocket of her sweats. She flipped it up and started responding.

I wiped Coke on my sleeve. "Care to share?"

"It's Rafael. He wants to come over. Do you mind?"

Did I mind? Of course, I minded. Ugh. Trying to weasel his way into our best friend time. "Doesn't he know you're busy?"

She blew air out of her nose. "Dude, we do this, like, every weekend."

I flopped back on the pile of pillows dramatically and clutched the bag of chips to my chest. "Fine. But he doesn't get to pick the movies or eat my chips."

She grinned. "Technically, those are my chips." She texted what I assumed was an affirmative answer. "He's going to bring JJ too. I think he kinda likes you."

"Excuse me, what? I thought we established I already have a boyfriend. I don't think I can handle two." How the hell did I go from zero prospects to two in the span of a few weeks? I guess when the most popular boy of your class decides you're girlfriend material, the other boys follow to see what the fuss is about. That was my hypothesis, anyway.

It wasn't long before we heard the murmur of voices from downstairs accompanied by a high-pitched laugh.

Then Mrs. James hollered up the stairs, "Bridget, honey, there are boys here."

Bridget hopped off the bed to shout back, "Thanks, Mom!"

The boys came trumping up the stairs, the suffocating smell of Axe Unlimited wafting in behind them. They were dressed similarly in hoodies, slouchy jeans, and sneakers. JJ had a brown sketchbook tucked up under his arm. Did this nerd bring homework?

"Salvatore."

"Esparza."

Bridget had her arms around his waist. "Behave, you two."

Rafael winked at me, and I scowled, which I'm sure gave him great joy. I had kept my mouth shut about him getting handsy at the Halloween party because I wasn't sure what difference it would make anyway. Bridget always seemed to forgive all his flaws.

His hand slid to the small of her back. "I'm always nice."

I stuck out my tongue like a petulant four-year-old and grabbed the remote to unpause the movie. Rafael whispered something in Bridget's ear, and JJ came to sit on my side of the bed. Were we just gonna all snuggle up here together?

JJ pulled a leg up and looked at me expectantly. He was all long limbs and elbows and cheekbones with thick black hair and fuzzy caterpillar eyebrows. He'd probably be good-looking when he finally grew into all of his body parts. The bed dipped when Bridget and Rafael sat down, her curled up against his chest and him snagging the Oreos.

"Hey," JJ said. It seemed I was not going to get to watch this movie after all. Not that it would be my first viewing, but whatever.

I popped open the bag of chips. "Chips?"

JJ smiled. "Yeah, sure." And stuck his big hand into the bag.

I tried to crane my head sideways so I could see around his head. He stayed facing me while he ate his handful of chips.

I sneaked a glance at Bridget. She was reclined against Rafael, one leg pulled up to her chest while the other rested on top. Her bare foot bopped slowly to a beat that definitely didn't belong to our movie. Raf was playing Snake on his phone. They both seemed painfully oblivious to the awkwardness happening on the other side of the bed.

How? Just...how?

JJ wiped chip dust on his jeans and cleared his throat. "So. Did you get your self-portraits done?"

"Yep." They were as done as they were gonna get. We'd have our critiques in class this week.

"Yeah, me too." He thumbed the edge of his sketchbook. "Hey, would you mind looking at something for me? It's not for an assignment, just something I did on my own, but I'd like to know what you think. You're really good. Definitely better than me." The tops of his cheeks pinked up.

I sat up straighter. "Yeah, sure."

His hands shook slightly as he fiddled with the book, getting to the right page. It kind of made me nervous. I wasn't sure what he was about to show me.

The covers fell open. "Like I said, just something random."

It was me.

I was definitely not expecting that.

And I looked...cute.

I don't know if he'd drawn the portrait from life or memory...I'm guessing memory since my shoulders were bare, and I couldn't remember a time when JJ would have ever seen me with bare shoulders. I was assuming he gave up on the clothes because he spent so much time on the face. My hair was pulled back in a loose ponytail, so heavy pieces framed my face. I was looking off to the side, wearing the tiniest of smiles. I think he was very generous with the structure of my cheekbones, but it still managed to look like me. He'd somehow managed to make me look hard and soft at the same time.

"Uh...it's...really nice." I wasn't sure if I should be flattered or worried.

Rafael suddenly leaned over. "Hey, JJ managed to make you look less like a bitch."

My face heated. "I need some water." I knocked the sketchbook off the bed in my haste to leave the room. I heard a flurry of voices in my wake; one of them was definitely Bridget whisper-shouting.

The only light left on downstairs was the little one in the hood above the stove and the outside light above the back porch. Mrs. James always left them on so we could get more snacks and so the boys could see when they snuck back out after the midnight curfew.

Footsteps behind me signaled that I had been followed.

"Hey, I'm sorry for the 'bitch' comment. I thought that was our shtick. You know, you call me names, I call you names, the Circle of Life goes on and all."

I ignored him and grabbed a glass from the cabinet, filling it with tap water.

"Are you really gonna be mad at me for that?"

I whirled. "No, I'm going to be mad at you for other things."

I couldn't see much of his eyes in the dark, but I could see his cocky-ass grin. "Like what?"

"Like groping me at the Halloween party. I still haven't told Bridget."

He shrugged. "I was really drunk."

"And that's a good excuse?"

He lifted his arm to run a hand through his shaggy hair, and up came his hoodie, exposing a striation of brown skin and dark hair. Not that I noticed. I took a sip of water.

"No," he said, "it's not an excuse. It's just what happened. I'm sorry. Are you going to apologize for punching me in the face?"

"No." Sip sip sip.

"Can we call a truce, then?" He held out a hand, and I smacked it away but gently.

"Why did you bring JJ here? Did you know he drew...that?" Me.

Rafael sighed and leaned up against the sink. He didn't bother to leave much room between us. "I didn't know about the picture. He had mentioned in passing that he might like you, you know, like that. And I am an excellent friend."

I rolled the glass between my palms. "Well, I'm taken."

"Well, you could do better."

"What's that supposed to mean?"

How, exactly, could I do better? London was a varsity football player. A varsity *quarterback* football player. I could literally get no higher in the social hierarchy chain. And he was super cute, too.

Rafael shrugged again.

"No, you can't just say crap like that and then not answer. London is nice."

He gave me a long, sidelong glance. "I'm sure you know him way better than me."

"I'm sure I do," I huffed. After all, we'd had one pseudo-date and one real date, and we talked almost every night on the phone until Mom yelled at me that she needed to use the computer for work.

"Just let him down easy, okay? It looked like he worked really hard on that picture."

"Are you saying I look good?"

He snorted. "I'm saying he made you look good, Salvatore."

Ah, we were back to normal now. I downed the rest of my water and set the glass down in the sink as gently as I could.

I turned around to head back upstairs, but somehow, Rafael had managed to position himself in front of me again. He wasn't that much taller than me but still had to look down. Which he was doing now.

What was left of the air between us heated suddenly, and it was so, so extremely weird. Like something was being left unsaid. I stared at the column of his throat, racking my brain for what I was supposed to be saying in this moment.

Yep, nothing.

Rafael broke the tension by coughing and sticking his hands in the pockets of his jeans, which did nothing to alleviate my sudden wandering gaze.

"We should probably get back," he said. "Before it gets weird."

Too late.

SIX

THE NEXT FEW DAYS in Art were awkward as hell.

Art was my longest class of the day because of lunch. So, it was an hour and a half of JJ shooting me covert glances. I had tried to let him down easy, but I think I accidentally left room for negotiation.

During the critique of our self-portraits, he piped up and called mine introspective and inspiring, which caused Mrs. Pearson to raise her eyebrows because JJ had yet to talk during a critique this year.

After our critiques, we were given our next assignment: multimedia self-portraits.

I was buried behind a stack of old National Geographics, cutting out brown and green landscapes to use for hair, when JJ decided to slide over to my table.

My table buddies were too absorbed in their own work to notice the new addition.

"Hey," he said, laying his materials out in front of him. I eyed his sketchbook like it was a venomous snake, waiting to ambush me with more pictures of my face.

"Hey," I replied. I kept working, scissors snicking easily through the silky paper.

"Mrs. Pearson is really on about self-portraits, huh?"

I waved the scissors. "Well, you know, self-reflection is all the rage these days. At least no one is cutting off ears yet."

He guffawed, startling my blonde table buddy, Rachel. I was not that funny.

Suddenly, Rachel gasped, and I found out the reason why a few seconds later when a pair of warm hands covered my eyes.

"Guess who?" London's warm breath fluttered against my ear.

He uncovered my eyes and pulled up an empty chair, spinning it around and plopping down backward, arms crossed over the back. It was so effortlessly cool. Rachel was openly staring, a slightly starstruck look on her face.

Art was one of those very relaxed classes, where students were free to come and go. Mrs. Pearson's tolerance of our fickle muses extended to the classroom. As long as the work got done, she didn't really mind where or when.

It wasn't unusual for there to be visitors to our classroom. I had never had a visitor before, though.

I glanced around for Mrs. Pearson anyway, but she was occupied at a different table.

"What are you working on?" London asked.

"Dude, we were talking."

"Dude, no one cares."

The dismissive tone of London's voice had me flinching internally. It was not something I'd heard from him before, and JJ's face flamed scarlet.

Rafael's warning echoed in my mind. *You could do better.* But I didn't care what Rafael thought, and JJ was his best friend, so of course he was on his side.

Still, JJ didn't deserve that.

I opened my mouth to reply, but London turned his megawatt smile on me, and any protest died immediately. My heart skittered. It felt good to be in the center of that infectious smile.

"C'mon. I have something to show you."

His hand closed around mine and gently tugged.

"What? Leave class? Right now?" I might be a menace to Sister Constance, but I had never skipped out on a class in my life. Skipping and getting deliberately kicked out were two very different things.

"Yeah. No one will notice."

He was probably right. Rachel was the only one besides me and JJ that had marked London's intrusion, and she had returned to her work. JJ was leaning as far away as possible now without physically leaving his chair.

"Um, okay."

I stacked my supplies in a tidy pile and then let London tug me out of the classroom.

We had just rounded the corner of the art hallway when I heard, "Sophia?"

Bridget's lilting voice stopped us both cold, me thumping into London's back. My stomach dropped out like I had been caught doing something wrong.

I turned slowly, attempting to be casual, like skipping class with my boyfriend was a totally normal day.

"Hey, Bridgey."

Bridget's fourth period was a study hall. She had a stack of manila folders and paper in her arms. She must have been running errands for the librarians again, which would explain why she was also out in the hallway during class.

Her sharp blue eyes flicked from me to London down to our clasped hands and back up again. "Are you skipping?"

"Uhh..."

"What? Are you her mother?"

Bridget's eyes narrowed dangerously, and I flinched with my face. No one, and I mean no one, spoke to Bridget James like that. London was in fine form today, not scoring brownie points with anyone.

Without a word, she turned on her heel, uniform skirt swishing, and marched in the other direction.

Suddenly, absconding with London did not seem like the best idea.

I didn't move to do anything, though, and continued to let him lead me out a set of doors that led to the courtyard.

Yes, we had a rather extensive courtyard filled with picnic tables, ringed with a low creek rock wall, with a view of the football field in the distance. Students were allowed to have lunch out here, and every once in a while, you'd get a cool teacher who brought class outside on a pretty day. Usually, it was the English teachers.

So, technically, since it was still lunch period, we hadn't broken any rules. Some of the picnic tables were even occupied.

"You wanted to show me the courtyard? I've seen the courtyard."

"No." He hoisted me up on the outer wall. "I wanted to show you this."

And then he kissed me, his lips warm in the slightly chilled November air.

We had been kissing a lot, but London didn't seem to be improving. I had to give him credit for enthusiasm, though. His tongue moved aggressively against mine.

And that's when I felt his hands on the sides of my bare thighs. It was November, cold enough for a branded green sweater but not for anything under my skirt. Which is why I could feel his fingers brushing against the hem of it.

It was enough to distract me from the kissing.

His fingertips sent tingles up and down my legs, but he didn't move them any farther.

We finally came up for air, my lips feeling swollen and chapped.

"Was that worth it?" he said.

I was starting to think it was...except without the distraction of his mouth on mine, the nervous feeling crept back into my gut.

"Hey, why did you have to say that to Bridget?"

His brow furrowed. "I thought you were mad at her."

"Dude, that was like, a week ago."

"Oh." He graced me with that dazzling smile. The one that made me feel like the only girl in the entire world. It felt nice to bask in the center of his attention. "I just wanted to be on your side."

Oh, well, that was nice. Wasn't it?

"He is not getting a blowjob."

I heard Bridget choke on the other end of the line. "Excuse me?"

I tucked the handheld tighter to my ear. I was upside down on my bed, legs propped up on the wall, watching the mint green polish dry on my toes.

"I do have some standards when it came to putting things in my mouth—brussels sprouts and penises are out."

She huffed a soft laugh. "I thought you were just dating."

"We are." London and I hung out regularly, held hands at school, and did other cutesy boyfriend/girlfriend activities that I used to make fun of other people for doing. "I mean, eventually, if we get that far." I shrugged, even though I knew she couldn't see me. "I just want to be prepared. Lay down some ground rules."

"You're supposed to lay down ground rules?" Based on the tone of her voice, I could tell she had her nose scrunched up.

"I don't know. Maybe?"

I was the one who had never had a boyfriend. What the hell did I know? She had Rafael; she was supposed to know more about these things.

"Do you want to have sex with him?"

I fell silent, pondering the choice I'd need to be making in the near future if London's handsy palming was any indication. Premarital sex was supposed to be a sin, but my mom had raised a liberal, free-thinking little Catholic —much to the dismay of Sister Constance if she ever found out.

I played with a strand of my hair, curling it meticulously around a finger. "I don't know. That's what's supposed to come next, right?"

I really wasn't sure, honestly. His kissing hadn't gotten any better, but I liked him, and we were dating. I was pretty sure sex was the next step.

"Sophia." Her voice was stern. "You do not have to have sex with him if you don't want."

"I know that." But I also knew girls got dumped for not putting out. It had happened to a couple girls on the team who started dating older guys. One girl had been so distraught, she skipped a week of school and missed two games, and she had been one of our strongest defenders. As a team, we could have murdered that boy.

Suddenly, loud country music started blaring from the back of the house. Mom's cleaning music.

Bridget must have heard it because she said, "Saturday spree?"

Bridget knew that Saturday mornings were reserved for cleaning, and it was only a matter of time before I was given a task. I was surprised I had been able to hide out undisturbed in my room for so long, even if it was under the pretense of folding my laundry, which was still just piled up on the end of the bed.

I sighed. "Yeah, I gotta go."

Bridget made a *hmmp*ing noise that indicated she clearly thought this conversation wasn't finished, but Saturday sprees were basically sacred in my house.

I had just clicked the "end" button when the doorbell rang.

"GET THAT."

We rarely ever got unexpected visitors to the house. It was either a politician or Mrs. Beal come to enlist our cooperation for the neighborhood yard sale.

I opened the door.

It was neither.

There was a man standing on our front porch. He was only a couple inches taller than me, with a dark, weathered face and a head full of curly hair just like mine, only his was streaked with silver. His big, bushy Italian eyebrows were, unfortunately, the same as mine as well.

He wore a soft leather bomber jacket—the one I used to roll around in when I was little because it smelled nice. He carried a battered suitcase.

"Hello, Sophia."

I slammed the door and locked it.

SEVEN

MY DAD LEFT WHEN I was about to be an eighth-grader, on the cusp of that awkward stage between middle and high school when you don't quite know what you want to be—an art kid or a jock—and you thought wearing a different colored bandana every day to school for a week counted as a fashion statement.

But "left" wasn't the right word. It was more like kicked-out because my mom finally got tired of dealing with his bullshit.

I was thirteen. It was the middle of June and sweltering. It was one of those nights, heavy with silence because nothing dared to breathe. I could hear the rhythmic click of the fan, the hum of the air conditioner, the occasional passing car. There was a loud thud as my father's body hit the floor. I got up to investigate in my frog pajamas, padding down the hallway to peek into the living room. Dad was face-down on the floor in a puddle of what looked like regurgitated oranges. The front door was wide open; moonlight slanted on the floor. Mom was crouched down beside him, her eyes black disks in her pale face. She'd ordered me back to my room, and I fled, jumping back into bed and pulling the covers over my head.

My father had been a sloppy drunk—the pass-out, incoherent, don't-think-they're-hurting-anybody-but-themselves kind. When your father had always been preoccupied with something else, it was easy to pretend he didn't exist. It was also easy to perpetuate this fantasy because he stopped showing up to public events when I was in the first grade. People just assumed my mom was single—which didn't sit too well with the upper-middle-class PTA moms—and everybody was too polite to ask otherwise.

I was in the seventh grade before I realized that, in fact, Dad was never going to show up. And that's when I stopped caring.

Of course, Mom had heard when I slammed the door. She came out in sweats with her hair pushed back by a headband. "Who was it?"

I stalked past her.

"Sophia, what—"

The doorbell rang again.

They were talking in Mom's bedroom—their bedroom again, I guess—with the door closed. Dad had left his suitcase in the living room. The vindictive part of me wanted to throw it outside. Instead, I put on a hoodie and threw myself outside in the backyard. I found a soccer ball, and it made a satisfying crack every time I kicked it against the fence.

He came out of the house about fifteen minutes after I started my little exercise and sat down on the edge of the patio. My face was sweaty, and my breath frosted in the air.

"I've missed you, Soph."

"Yeah." Crack. Crack. Crack.

"And Mom. It's been hard being away. But I had to go. I couldn't let you or Cele fight my demons anymore."

Crack.

"But I've found my way back. The Lord has led me back into the light, and every sober day, I bask in His glory."

"I'm sure."

"Will you look at me, please?"

I gave the ball one last good kick at the fence; it hit a knot in one of the slats and bounced into the garden.

I looked. He was older, so much older, than the last time I saw him. His face was droopy, his shoulders slumped. A tiny husk of a man. "What do you want me to see, Dad?"

"God has saved me, Sophia. Forgiven my trespasses. I hope, maybe, you can too."

When I didn't answer, he nodded as if confirming something to himself. And maybe he was.

How was I supposed to argue when he threw around shit like that?

We stared at each other for the longest minute of my life, my breath coming hot and furious.

I heard the back door swing open again, and Mom walked out. She'd added an oversized, knit cardigan to her mess of a Saturday spree outfit. She sat down next to Dad on the steps, pulling the sides closed.

It was a familiar gesture as the cardigan was her favorite. During the winter months, and sometimes even in the summer, I'd see her put that cardigan on, pull the sides tight, and bury her nose in the sleeves.

That's when the pieces started clicking uncomfortably into place.

It wasn't an oversized cardigan. It was a man's.

The late-night phone calls she denied. The one-sided whispers I'd heard coming from the other side of her closed door.

Mom slipped her hand into the crook of his arm.

Seeing them together again caused a flood of memories to rush through me, most of them unpleasant.

Our scarce family vacations ending in tears and yelling because Dad got drunk on the beach.

Family dinners ruined because Dad forgot what shift he was on, forgot to pick up the milk, the takeout, or me up from practice.

That last one was fun.

I honestly couldn't drudge up a memory of the three of us that didn't include Mom yelling or crying.

"Sophia, I wanted to talk to you before your dad got here." She slid him A Look, but he just patted her like there was nothing wrong. Finally, a familiar dynamic. He hadn't even been back an hour and had already pissed Mom off.

"I was excited." He laughed.

I scowled.

Mom looked like she was holding back a sigh. "Your dad and I have been talking for a while. He wanted to come home and put our family back together."

Oh, great.

EIGHT
December 2005

MOM STARTED BUYING RICE Crispies again since they were Dad's favorite. Before I was old enough to realize that cereal couldn't talk, I would spend breakfast interpreting the snap, crackle, and pops for my dad.

These days, while Mom was making her coffee, Dad would come into the kitchen, peck her cheek, put his hand on the small of her back, and say, "What a beautiful day the Lord has made." Sitting in my spot at the counter, I barely resisted the urge to vomit or drown myself in the cereal bowl.

Since Dad had come back just in time for the holidays, I did not have school as an escape. I had to find other ways to avoid my house. I clung to Bridget like a barnacle. We went to the mall at least once a week during break. Even when I wasn't with her, I told my parents I was. I picked up extra hours at Eaton's Drug Store. I was the _____ __ arrive and last to leave for all our indoor games and consistently forgot to tell Mom and Dad when they were.

On Sundays, Dad would knock on my door at 8:30 and ask if I wanted to go to church. You would think after the first three, "No thanks, I get enough religion," he would give up and leave me the hell alone. But no. He'd faithfully show up in a button-down shirt and tie, trying to save my soul. It was like looking at your reflection in a funhouse mirror; all the basic parts were there, but the image was distorted. Grotesque.

I was woken up very abruptly, and very early, one morning by someone insistently poking my butt. "Sophia, get up."

Mom was bustling around my room, picking up dirty clothes. I mumbled incoherently and pulled the comforter over my head.

She jerked the covers away and threw a pair of sweatpants on my face. "Hurry up. Your dad wants to take you shopping."

I didn't move. "For what?"

"Does it matter?"

"Yeah."

She leaned in close, and I shrunk deep into the pillows. "Sophia Irene, you have five minutes to get out of this bed.

Your dad is making the effort, and so will you."

I got up and dressed immediately. I knew it was serious business when she started throwing around my middle name.

Dad was all cheery smiles when I came into the living room. "Ready, little bit?" He hadn't called me "little bit" since I was five.

I hitched on a pleasant expression. "Yep."

I was ready, but I was also a hot mess in a matching sweater and sweatpants, Aggies '07 emblazoned in green across my boobs and down my leg. I was behind on my laundry.

"Great!" I thought he was overdoing it just a bit. "Let's go."

He led the way to the car, me dragging my feet along in his wake. His car was exactly as I remembered, beige — Dad was a beige man—with the same dent in the bumper I'd made at eleven with my bike. He opened the door for me before going over to his own side. "I figured we'd stop at the mall first. Then we can get some lunch after. Buckle up."

I did, trying not to get myself child-locked. Dad's car tended to do that. "Um, what are we shopping for?"

"A Christmas present for Mom." He put the car into reverse, looking into the mirror.

"I've already got Mom a present." I'd gotten her a thick silver bracelet with turquoise and silver beads. Bridget had helped me pick it out.

"Oh." He laughed. "I forget how fast you kids grow up. Remember when you used to call me on my way home from work on Christmas Eve crying because you didn't have a present for her?" He laughed again, shaking his head. "I always had you covered, didn't I?"

"Yeah." I looked out the window.

"Well, if you see anything you like, I'll get it for you."

Dad didn't talk much after that, and I talked less.

The mall was chaotic as it was only four days until Christmas. Any other time, we would have been back in the car before you could say, "run for your lives." Dad hated crowds just as much as I did. Instead, he dragged me through every store that had even the remotest feminine tilt to it. We browsed through froufrou lotions and soaps, clothes, jewelry, shoes, and even a nauseatingly smelly candle shop.

We left about four hours later, arms full of loot. I was exhausted. Dad was worse than Bridget if that were possible. At least she would take breaks every once in a while at the food court so she could get ogled. Dad was jabbering excitedly about our purchases. He'd gotten a whole basket of lotion and body wash in Mom's favorite scent—which I had to pick out—and a horrid ruffled blouse. Dad had insisted she would love it. I knew it would end up in a pile at the back of her closet in about a month. Just enough time for him to forget.

On our way to the exit, we had the misfortune of running into Rafael. He looked as startled to see me as I was to see him. There was an awkward few seconds where the three of us just stared at each other.

"Uh, hi," I said.

Raf dug his hands deep into his pockets. "Hey."

Dad cleared his throat. "Sophia, are you going to introduce me to your friend?"

Noooooooo.

Dad waited expectantly.

"Dad, this is Rafael from school," I ground out, barely.

They shook hands—who even does that anymore?—and then Dad said it was a pleasure to meet him, and Raf said it was cool.

Someone kill me.

"Well, we have to go, bye." And then I fled, hoping Dad had enough sense to follow me and not linger.

Safely back on the road again, we headed in the general direction of home.

"What do you feel like eating?"

My stomach rumbled in anticipation. "I don't care. Whatever."

He smiled at me, but he had put his sunglasses on, and I couldn't tell if it reached his eyes or if he was finally as tired of this charade as I was. I could only see my own tired reflection in the lenses of the dark aviators, which were infinitely cooler than he was.

What I had in mind was more like a McDonald's, but Dad picked a fancy restaurant with ambiance lighting and vinyl menus.

"This is nice," he said, right after we ordered, lacing his fingers together on the tabletop.

"Um. Yeah, it is." I helped myself to some complimentary bread.

It was weird to see him nursing nothing stronger than unsweetened iced tea with lemon. Before, when we went out to dinner as a family, he'd order Old Fashioneds until his eyes were glassy and Mom couldn't look at him anymore. She'd flash sharp apologetic smiles at our waitresses every time he waved his hand around for another one.

"So, Rafael was handsome."

Oh, baby Jesus, no.

"Sophia, listen." He paused and tried to frown and stalled, appearing as if he was trying to find the right words. "I know that...when you reach a certain age—"

I stopped playing with the bread. This was all Rafael's fault. "Dad, don't."

"At a certain age," he continued as if I hadn't spoken, "you want to start experimenting. Finding out about stuff."

"I don't need this talk." He must have interpreted our earlier encounter as the awkwardness surrounding a girl crush instead of the shock of seeing your nemesis in a place you didn't expect him to be.

Dad stared at me, and I swallowed. I could see his teeth worrying the inside of his bottom lip. It wasn't something I expected a man of his age to do. "There's a youth group at church that deals with these sorts of topics led by a very nice man, Father Adrian Bailey."

"I'm not going to some damn youth group."

"I know I haven't been the best...role model."

"Would you just drop it?"

Dad's mouth snapped shut with an audible click of teeth.

In the quiet, I heard his tennis shoes shuffle against the carpet. The waitress brought our food, and I dropped my eyes to my plate, feeling the heat on my face. It was totally his fault he didn't know about Father Adrian and Rafael and London and everything else. That's just what happened when you weren't around.

I tried not to feel guilty for being short with him, but guilt churned my stomach anyway. He was trying, after all. But I had very little patience for him swooping back into my life, pretending he knew anything about me.

Christmas day dawned bright and sunny, even though there was a fine layer of fresh snow coating the ground. It was the first time we'd had snow on Christmas in several years, and that phenomenon alone got me excited enough to get up and press my face against my bedroom window to watch it fall.

When I finally decided to wander into the living room, I was immediately taken aback by the scene presented before me.

It was disconcerting, seeing them cozied up on the couch together, each cradling a mug of coffee and basking in the lights from the tree like they used to do when I was little. The last Christmas I remember Dad attending, he was propped up in the chair, tipping a bottle of Jack into his coffee, his liquor-laugh coating everything.

I tried not to grimace and made a lot of noise entering the room, trying to startle them into unsticking.

My plan failed.

Dad just put his hand possessively on Mom's knee and gave me a toothy grin. "There you are, Soph! We were starting to think you'd sleep Christmas morning away."

They shared a laugh that seemed to say, "Oh, teenagers!"

Dad seemed unusually excited, but I guess that was expected for his first Christmas as part of the family again.

I took up my usual spot under the tree and started sorting through the presents; I couldn't seem to muster the same sort of giddy excitement that normally accompanied this day. My stack of presents was always the biggest, but lately Mom had been exchanging quantity for quality—less glitter nail polish and more business casual blouses.

Most of the presents had a tag that read *From: Mom & Dad*, so I was surprised when I found one that just read *From: Dad*.

He was fidgeting enthusiastically in his seat. "Go on. Open that one first."

I tore through the creatively wrapped package—it was obvious that mom hadn't wrapped this one—and found in my hands a book. *Submitting to Jesus: A Girl's Guide to Loving Christ*, to be exact. By H. Miriam Trent, PhD.

"What is this?" I held the book gingerly by the tips of my fingers as if it'd bite me any second.

"Dr. Trent was one of the group leaders at the center. She's really a wonderful Godly woman with three daughters. You've been so distant lately...I thought you might need some guidance."

"Guidance," I repeated flatly. "You think I'm the one with the problem?"

Dad flushed, and Mom put her hand on his arm. "Michael, I really think Sophia's old enough to make her own choices."

I made an affirmative snort which was quickly misinterpreted.

"Sophia, enough."

"I'm making an effort here, Sophia, and I'd appreciate it if you'd meet me halfway."

"You're about four years too late."

"Sophia, if I learned one thing while I was away, it's this: it's never too late."

"Did H. Miriam Trent tell you that?"

"Young lady—"

"God may forgive you, but that doesn't mean I have to." I tossed the book to the ground and left the rest of my presents unopened.

I did know how to make an exit.

I could feel my face grow hot and tight with the pressure of unshed tears, but I swore off crying over him years ago.

Burrowing into my comforter, I pulled Sir Bearington the bear from under my pillows—who was practically bald from my affections—and pressed him to my face.

It wasn't long before I heard a click, and then I was joined on the bed. Judging by the feathery touch along my back, it was my mom.

"Your dad is really trying here."

"I think I prefer drunk dad to Jesus dad."

"He's changed, Sophia. He genuinely believes everything he's saying."

I rolled over to face her, Bearington still clutched in my arms. She wasn't looking at me; more like staring wistfully at the wall where my Backstreet Boys poster hung, a huge Sharpied heart around Nick Carter's face.

"You believe all that crap?"

She patted my hand absently. "Sometimes, that's the only thing we can do."

NINE

December 2005/January 2006

THERE WAS ONLY ONE thing that could alleviate the boredom and suffering of Christmas vacation: Bridget James's New Year's Eve party. It was an event hosted mainly by her parents, Shelley and Keith, for their work friends and some relatives who lived in the vicinity, but every year, Bridget got to invite her own friends. It was entertaining enough. Inevitably a middle-aged aunt would get hammered and hit on one of the high school boys Bridget had brought.

I had always thought of this event as one of my civic best friend duties, a distraction, so all the attention and probing questions were not focused solely on Bridget. But that was before. This time, I had a date. A nice piece of arm candy that was sure to attract the appreciation of any nosy relatives (and probably a hammered aunt or two). I was practically bubbling over with excitement.

I used the guilt money Mom had given me to make up for Dad's debacle of a Christmas gift to purchase a strapless red dress with tulle underskirt. The tulle was already itching the backs of my thighs, but I cut quite a figure in the dress, and it was worth it.

London was picking me up at eight thirty p.m. I stood by the door, huddled in my coat, ready to dart out at the slightest glimpse of headlights. Mainly, I stood there because it was the farthest I could get from my parents without actually standing outside. Mom was on the couch, and Dad was in the chair, still sniping across the coffee table about my curfew. I'd never had a curfew. I told Mom where I was going, who I was with, and my expected time home, and she was good. When I'd informed my father that I was curfew-less, he'd gone all apoplectic, and Mom'd shot me dirty looks. Apparently, good girls had decent curfews and were not allowed to gallivant freely all night long. They had argued about it the entire time I was getting ready and had still not reached a consensus.

They were still bickering when I saw London's truck round the corner.

"Mom," I said, hand on the doorknob. "Mom. Mom."

"Yes, Sophia." She broke away, and Dad lapsed into glowering silence.

"I'm just going to spend the night at Bridget's," I said.

"That's fine." Her eyes slid back to my father. Neither of them spoke. I thought I saw her eyes narrow. Maybe it was a twitch. Maybe it was just the lighting. Maybe she was finally seeing what I saw.

"You look pretty," said London.

We were idling in his truck outside Bridget's house, letting frost collect on the windows. I felt his warm hand slide over my knee. I smiled in the dim light of a street lamp and took his hand.

"We have to go in."

He laughed and leaned closer, his hot breath fluttering over my neck. "Nah. We have time."

It was tempting. Oh, so tempting. His body was warm next to mine, and he smelled delicious. His fingers twined in a strand of my hair.

I smacked him away playfully. "Stop it. You can't mess up my hair before people get to see it."

He laughed again and retreated to a safe distance. "Come on, then." He took my hand. "Let's go show you off."

The décor was confetti, and strands of twinkle lights roped over Mrs. James' expensive trinkets. The woman herself greeted us at the door, resplendent in a champagne and glitter cocktail dress, a "Happy New Year" hat perched on her head.

"Sophia, darling! So glad you could make it!" She grabbed me with her cherry-red talons and pulled me into a crushing hug.

"Thanks for inviting us, Mrs. James," I said into her armpit.

She released me, patting my hair. "Any time, dear. And who is this?" I thought for a moment she was going to grab London into a hug as well, but he forestalled her with a handshake.

"This is my boyfriend, London Hart." My stomach flip-flopped with joy at the label.

"I've heard so much about you." She shuffled us inside. "Let me have your coats. Bridget and the others are in the den."

I threaded my fingers through London's, and we started to maneuver our way to the back of the house. I said "Hello" to the relatives I did know, throwing around the title of "my boyfriend" with abandon. We snagged some punch from the kitchen—London only got groped once—and found ourselves in the den. The den was a stuffy room, paneled in dark wood with dark furniture. It was a stereotypical man's room—dark and quiet.

We stepped into the silence, and it only took me a moment to deduce what had happened. The room was split almost evenly between boys and girls. Shelby, Emma, and a few of the other girls from the team were piled on the couch. Shelby gave me a wide-eyed look filled with significance. Rafael and his gang of friends—Dean, JJ, and Matt—were huddled on the opposite side, passing around a bottle. JJ had been giving me the cold shoulder ever since that day in Art.

Bridget's ridiculously high blonde bouffant suddenly filled my vision, and she latched onto my free hand.

"Sophianeedtalknow." Her lips were in a tight line, even though sounds were coming out of her mouth fast and furious.

I blinked. "What?"

Before she could repeat the gibberish, Rafael had joined us at the door.

"Well, well. If it isn't Sophia Salvatore."

Bridget's eyes rolled so hard, I saw a scary expanse of white and felt like I was in an Exorcist movie. Any second now, she was going to projectile vomit all over the upholstery.

Raf didn't even look at her. It was as I thought; Romeo and Juliet had been fighting again. His pupils were huge, and he reeked of cigarettes and cheap Eau de Asshole. Raf unscrewed the cap of the bottle he carried and held it up, meaning clear.

Bridget huffed loudly and stormed off to find a more sympathetic ear.

One sniff from the bottle singed my nose hairs, but both London and I let him spike our punch. Raf smiled, eyes out of focus. "Let's get this party started." He took a swig of the dark liquid.

The party escalated quickly; Raf seemed to have an endless supply of bottles to pull out of a gray backpack. Currently, he had his head out the window, JJ holding onto his waistband. Someone had turned up the music, and we were dancing—bellies warm with whisky and adolescence hormones. London had his arms tight around me. We were barely moving, busy propping each other up. His hands trailed over my lower back and the top of my ass. He'd grown increasingly handsy over the past half-hour. I wiggled and giggled—a very girly and very drunk sound. It was as if we were the only two people in the room, and the others were getting quite a show.

His cheek pressed against mine. "Let's go somewhere."

My whole body warmed at the touch of his breath against my ear...and it had nothing to do with the alcohol.

I thought of all the places we could go and not get caught...probably. The list was a short one because all the more obvious places were out, seeing as the house was stuffed full of randoms. But there was one place—a cold and deserted part of the basement that had been left out during the remodel. We smoked pot in there once.

I grabbed London's hand, and we stumbled to the door and tried sneaking out quietly, quite a feat considering I was snickering uncontrollably. If anyone noticed, they were considerate enough not to say anything, at least until tomorrow. Our absence would be marked and categorized with all the superior detective skills of six teenage girls.

Hauling London through the house, we managed to avoid any adults who knew us by name. We slipped into the basement with all the grace and subtlety of two horny elephants. Our destination was an unfinished cell of a room; exposed two-by-fours for walls, a moth-eaten couch, a couple wobbly chairs, and a busted TV were all that was left of the furniture.

London's mouth was on mine with an intense, sloppy urgency I'd never felt before. His teeth clacked against mine, and he bit my lip. We stumbled to the couch together, tripping over an errant footstool and landing with an *oof*. I might have let out a very unladylike grunt and then laughed.

London stopped, one hand on my boob, one tangled in my hair.

"You okay?" He was breathless.

"Yeah, yeah." I grabbed his head to stop it spinning and pulled him down.

He slipped a condom from his pocket and ripped the package with his teeth, spitting the silver debris on the floor.

There was a lot of mindless groping, heavy breathing, a moan or two from London, and then it was over. Slam, bam, thank you, ma'am. I didn't even lose any of my clothes. My stockings ended up around my ankles while my dress was rucked up around my hips. I was almost suffocating under London's spent weight—still on top of me—while the toes dangling over the edge of the couch were decidedly chilly.

"I love you." He nuzzled closer, head buried in my chest.

I felt special walking onto the field before a game. Crisp uniform, sleek (okay, mostly fuzzy, but sometimes sleek) ponytail, buffed leather cleats, thighs taut, and powerful.

Safe and protected in the cocoon of my teammates. I felt special every time I got to add a patch to my varsity jacket.

Wasn't the right boy—The One—supposed to make you feel special? Why didn't I feel anything? Wasn't it every girl's dream to have her dreamy, perfect boyfriend whisper "I love you" into her boobs? So, why then was I different?

Several days after New Year's, I stood in front of the bathroom mirror in shorts and sports bra, trying to see if losing my virginity had wrought any visible changes on my body. My bottom lip was still slightly swollen from London's overzealous amorous attentions. Nothing else that I could see. No bright eyes, no rosy cheeks, no seductive tilt of the mouth, no post-coital glow at all. Just me.

The door cracked open.

"Mom! Don't you knock?" My mom poked her head around the door. "What if I was doing something personal?"

"Lock the door, then. London's on the phone."

I tried not to grimace as I took the handheld. I had been studiously avoiding the boy. I sat on the toilet and braced myself for anything or nothing.

"Hey."

"Hey, baby. Haven't heard from you in a while."

"Yeah, you know, been busy."

"Whatcha been up to?"

"You know, stuff."

"Baby, you okay?" Baby. Baby. Baby.

"I'm fine. Just getting ready to go meet the girls. Can't talk long."

"Sophia, you can talk to me."

I drew circles on my knee with a fingernail. His voice sounded pleading. Say something. Say something. Say something.

"I know. I'll see you at school on Monday."

"Okay." Dejected deflation. "Love you."

"Okay. Bye."

We hung up—or, I hung up.

Shelby met me at the Wal-Mart in athletic sweats and an oversized hoodie, just like me. I had called her as soon as I had gotten rid of London. We wandered through the health and beauty section, fingertips trailing over eyeshadow and exfoliates.

Shelby broke the silence first like I trusted her to do. "What's wrong?"

"I had sex with London." There. I said it. Like ripping off a Band-Aid.

Her expression was shocked, then puzzled. Not quite the reaction I was expecting. "When?"

"New Year's."

She laughed. "So that's where you two went. Rafael owes JJ fifteen bucks."

"For what?" I picked up a particularly garish shade of purple and rolled it around in my hands.

"The boys all made bets about what you guys were up to. Raf said you were too stuck up to give it up. His words!" she added defensively after the nasty look I shot her.

"That stupid prick."

"How was it?"

"Um...fine, I guess."

"Fine? That's it?" She shrugged. "I wouldn't know, but I think it should be better than 'fine.'"

"Annnd then he told me he loved me."

She stopped fondling the lip glosses. "No, he didn't. What did you say?"

"Nothing...yet."

"What are you going to do?"

"I don't know. I should feel something, right? Maybe I'm broken. I'm a broken girl." A broken girl who couldn't help but think that this didn't feel right.

"You're not broken. You're—"

She stopped. We had stumbled into the family planning aisle, and I had my hand on a pregnancy test. "Sophia, you're not. You can't be. You used a condom, right?" Her voice had lowered to a whisper as if someone would walk past and overhear us.

"Of course we did. I took freshman health just like everybody else. I'm just double-checking." My sloshed brain hadn't even registered that London had come prepared for the evening's festivities as if he knew what was going to happen. But maybe he was always prepared. "Even abstinence is only 99.99% effective!" I added. Growing up Catholic had put the fear of Immaculate Conception deep in all of us. Half of the girls in our class had a pregnancy scare before they even started having sex.

She frowned. "This is not funny. If you get pregnant, Coach will kick you off the team, and we're almost seniors."

"I'm not. And if I am, you can have the honor of pushing me down the stairs. Deal?"

That forced a smile out of her. She knocked me in the arm. "C'mon. Let's get out of here before somebody sees us, or you'll be knocked up Monday morning anyway."

"Agreed."

If one of our classmates happened to catch a glance of me buying a pregnancy test, the rumor mill would start churning like nobody's business. I held the pregnancy test as covertly as possible without looking like I was stealing. We shuffled up to the self-checkout and made a beeline for the door, for once trying to draw no eyes our way.

The boys from Tangelo Park were a bunch of whiny bitches.

They started losing early, and then the fouling started. I'm pretty sure my ribs were going to be bruised from where one of their defenders slammed me into the wall.

Bridget and I limped off the field after we'd given the boys as much as we got, Joely patting both of us on the back. "Excellent work, ladies."

I sat on the bench with a groan and began undressing.

The indoor league was purely recreational and only partly optional. Joely expected us to stay conditioned over the off-season, and kicking the asses of a bunch of varsity boys' teams was the most entertaining way to do it.

I peeled off my sweaty shin guards and grinned at the Tangelo players that slumped by. The endorphins were pumping hard.

"Ice that ankle, James. I can't have you come back gimpy."

Bridget gave a tired nod of assent. I understood how she was feeling; it was our last indoor game and our last weekend before school started back up again. Then it was back to the grass field, crisp, white lines, and another shot at being District champs for the last time.

Bridget plopped her injured leg across my knees.

"Gross."

"Oh, please, please."

She leaned back on her hands while I rummaged in my bag for the prewrap and athletic tape. Her slender calf was sticky from her socks.

"Wiggle your toes."

She rolled her eyes but complied, signature pink phalanges wiggling.

I unrolled some of the prewrap and began my task, starting at the delicate arch of her foot. "I think you'll live."

I glanced up, but she looked a million miles away.

I nudged her. "Don't look so damn morose."

She gave me a weak smile. "I'll miss this. We're almost seniors, you know."

I finished the tape job quickly, giving her leg a quick pat when I was done. She flexed the ankle experimentally to make sure the tape wasn't too tight and then slipped into her flip-flops.

I pulled a pair of sweats over my shorts and stuffed my gear into my much-abused Saint Aggies green soccer bag. "Don't remind me."

The other girls were shuffling out with their parents—mine hadn't been invited—some stopping to chit-chat with Joely.

"Oh, look, the boys are here."

I looked up sharply, almost cricking my neck. Sure enough, Rafael and London were standing at the large double doors of the complex, not speaking to each other. Raf seemed extremely interested in the field hockey game in progress on the second field.

"What have you done?" I growled.

"What?" She pouted. "I thought it would be fun to double."

I attempted to smooth out my ponytail, collecting the sweaty flyways that escaped during the game.

"Rafael agreed to that?"

"Uh...not really." Ah, so that explained the awkward shuffling.

London finally spotted us and waved enthusiastically.

"Hey, you ride with London, and we'll meet you at Tony's diner, yes?"

We hefted our bags and began walking to the entrance. "Yeah, I guess."

She beamed. I did not share her enthusiasm. She must've thought she was doing me a big favor by letting me ride with my boyfriend, who I had not seen since he professed his love.

London greeted me with a kiss and a chivalrous hand on my bag. I glared at Bridget's flouncing ponytail all the way to the parking lot.

"You played great tonight."

"You watched?"

"I caught the end."

I grunted in response.

He put a hand, rather possessively, I thought, on my thigh, and I longed to wriggle away. Unfortunately, there was nowhere else to go in the cab of his small truck without making it super obvious I was trying to shake him off.

"I've missed you."

"I've been busy. Training and stuff."

"You've been distant."

"I'm just tired."

"We don't have to go. I'll take you home."

"No, it's fine."

I could tell he wanted to stay something else because he started chewing the inside of his cheek and his fingers tapped fretfully on the wheel. I could tell he wanted to ask questions. Questions I wasn't ready to answer. Maybe I didn't even know the answers.

I grabbed his hand and squeezed. "Really, it's fine. We wouldn't want to disappoint Bridget."

He squeezed back. "Whatever you say, babe."

Things didn't get any less awkward when we joined Bridget and Rafael in the diner.

Honestly, I think the awkwardness just got worse once we sat down and ordered. Bridget was overly bright and cheery, and London seemed to feed off her energy, so he became more obnoxious. Raf slouched in the booth, one arm slung over the back. I stuffed my face with cheese-covered tater tots.

I did not miss the covert glances Bridget was shooting Rafael or the glassy cast to her eyes. They must've argued on the way over—bet she regretted ditching me now!

She leaned over the table and touched London's arm while she laughed, the sound filling the small diner and drawing the eyes of several of the other, older patrons.

Wait a minute. Was she *revenge* flirting with *my* boyfriend?

I choked on a tot.

London turned to me, the epitome of concern, and started patting my back and cooing like I was an invalid.

"I need to pee."

I didn't need to pee; the atmosphere around the table was just suffocating.

Tony was familiar with the teens of Oxcreek and our group, so it was easy enough to head towards the bathroom and slip out the back door instead. It's not like the place was armed.

Tony's was squished between Eaton's and a drive-thru liquor store, so the back alley wasn't offensively smelly. Asphalt eventually gave way to a grassy lawn and a gravel road that led to the 4-H office.

The night was crisp and clear, so clear I could see the stars sprinkled about like glitter. Not that I could name any. I wondered how long I could stay out here before Bridget came to investigate what was taking so long.

I heard the heavy metal door creak—right on cue.

I turned around, an excuse ready on my tongue, but it wasn't Bridget.

It was Rafael Esparza.

"What are you doing here?"

"It's a free country."

He walked toward me, kicking gravel pieces with the toe of his high-tops. He pulled something from the pocket of his jacket and offered it to me, palm up.

A lighter and a thin white joint.

"You wanna hit this?" He drawled like maybe he'd already been hitting it. Maybe that's why Bridget was upset; she only liked to smoke on her time and her terms. I was very much like her in that regard. Even now, my stomach was fluttering anxiously at being so exposed.

"Scared, Salvatore?"

My frantically pounding heart said, *you betcha*.

My mind said, *yes*.

But my traitorous mouth said, "Not on your life, Esparza."

He grinned and pressed the joint to his lips but didn't light up. "Relax, Salvatore. I wouldn't endanger your perfect life. You can stop looking shifty."

I had to consciously stop myself from glancing around for witnesses.

"My life's not perfect." The thought was muttered, but Rafael heard anyway.

"Oh?"

I eyed the joint, almost tempted to take it and get caught. Getting caught in a dark alley behind a grimy diner smoking pot with a boy would be a sure-fire way to piss off new Jesus-Dad. I'm sure he assumed good girls never did stuff like that.

"You're thinking hard. Something you'd like to get off your chest, Salvatore?" His gaze had fallen to my boobs; hidden behind a sports bra and hoodie, they were nevertheless obviously visible.

"God, you're a fucking pervert."

He found that extremely funny, the joint almost falling as he laughed.

"No, wait." He grabbed my hand to prevent an epic storm-off. "Sorry. I was being serious."

Rafael? Serious? That was new and unexpected.

"Like I would tell you."

"I'm actually wiser than I look."

I snorted. "You're gonna have to prove that."

He flashed his pearly whites again. "Let me."

And wouldn't you just know it—that's when the back door slammed open for the second time.

There was a "What the fuck?" exclamation and then a quieter, husky "Sophia?" and I'm not sure which one said what, but judging by the look on Bridget's face, she was the foul mouth.

I realized about .2 seconds too late that my fingers and Rafael's were still entwined—when did that happen? —

and I jerked away like he'd bit me.

There was a hiss as the lighter flared, and then Rafael was taking a long drag off the joint. The sweet and pungent fragrance of marijuana filled the air, and Bridget's lip curled. "What are you doing?"

I made a quick decision and snatched the joint from between Raf's fingers. "What's it look like?" It was either that or admitting that we were...what? Talking? Except Rafael and I didn't talk.

I took a perfunctory puff and offered the joint to Bridget.

She ignored me, addressing Rafael instead. "I'm ready to leave."

Then she was gone in a swish of blonde hair and indignation.

Rafael shrugged and followed her, leaving me with the illegal paraphernalia and a silent London, whose expression I couldn't quite read. But it looked like a mixture of confusion and disappointment.

I licked my fingers and stubbed out the joint, stowing it away in my pocket for another time. "Yeah, let's go."

TEN

January 2006

IT WAS EASY AVOIDING London the first day back after Christmas vacation. We shared no classes this semester, and I spent an inordinate amount of time ducking in and out of the girls' bathrooms during breaks. After school, we both had our separate conditioning practices at separate ends of the school. Plenty of distance.

We huddled in our locker room, fresh-faced and jittery, swapping presents and stories from over break. I was squashed on a bench between Shelby and Tasia, sharing a magazine. Coach Joely entered the locker room, stiff-legged and golden bronze, Captain Bridget by her side. The room was silenced immediately. Bridget stared us all down—one by one—with flinty eyes. Her sleek blonde hair was swept up in her signature high ponytail that pulled her face into hard lines. Fierce.

"Ladies," Joely said, "last season was a disappointment."

Even though Coach wasn't looking at me, I felt "disappointment" stab through the tenderest parts of me — a physical force. I was the disappointment. And everyone knew about the superstar who choked at the first district game and fucked the season for the team. Tasia's leg twitched against mine.

"We have to be the fastest, the strongest, the most conditioned. Weight room Monday, Wednesday, and Friday at four with Saturday practice at seven a.m." There was a collective round of groaning. "No skipping, no complaining. I will cut you. And we'll be electing team captain at the spring sports banquet."

Bridget graced us with a dazzling smile, her whole body relaxing into malleable softness, born to the position.

Some girls balk at the idea of running. Dread it, really. They think of it as the most uncreative form of conditioning: boring, routine, purposeless. I happened to agree with them.

Ceaseless forward momentum without an end goal in mind, movement for the sake of movement...I just didn't get it. Give me a target. An opponent. Some uppity freshman girl with her jersey too tight and her hair too smooth that I could knock over. I liked having resistance. Something to achieve. Something to fight. Opposition, I understood.

What I loved was the weight room. Pitching my will and my body against the machines, pushing harder—always pushing. I thought of nothing except my shoes against the rubber pads of the leg press, watching my chunky thighs go taut with every repetition, doing anything and everything I asked of them.

I was lost in the pavement, the ache in my calves, and the thumping of my running playlist, so I didn't notice London's smoke-gray truck rumbling around the street until he'd pulled up beside me. The passenger window rolled down, and I could hear him calling my name.

Even in my own neighborhood on a Sunday morning, I was not safe. He'd found me at last.

I slowed down, pulling my headphones off and letting them settle around my neck, pressing Pause on my iPod that was strapped to my bicep.

"Are you stalking me?" I asked, forcing my tone to be light and airy. I pulled in cool air through my nose.

"Are you avoiding me?" I was a blank canvas, an emotionless fortress of calm. London cut the engine and leaned over to open the passenger door. "Get in."

I climbed in and waited.

He just stared at me, his face so young and undefined and touched slightly red. "Do you wanna break up?"

"London, no!"

"Then what? What do you want? Because I can't help the way I feel, Sophia. Life is too short for lies and half-truths, and I'm telling you the truth."

I knew what he wanted, so why was it so hard for me to give it to him? Emma loved a new boy every week. Bridget loved Rafael. Shelby loved Jesus. I loved bacon. It wasn't that hard.

"I love you," I blurted, pretending he was bacon.

His face relaxed into an easy smile, happy and content.

I slid over to his lap, sweat-slicked legs slipping over his, and kissed him full on the mouth with everything I had. His fingers crawled at my waistband, and I knew I had fixed us for now.

We ended up having sex in his truck in broad daylight, and it was the most awkward three minutes of my life. The windows hadn't quite fogged up like they did in *Titanic*, and even now, they were unthawing. London sat behind the wheel, messing around with his zipper while I fixed my shorts. Our clothes hadn't come all the way off— again. Which I guess was a blessing, considering where we were. Maybe no one noticed the truck parked in the cul-de-sac with the foggy windows.

There wasn't much talking happening, but I guess London had gotten what he came for, so he didn't have anything else to say. I felt...weird. Was this what people in love did?

"Hey," he finally said, starting the engine. "Do you want me to drop you off at home?"

My hand was already on the door handle, popping it open. "No, I'm going to finish my run."

I slipped out of the truck.

"Okay, later."

And he rumbled off as soon as I shut the door. What, no "I love you" this time?

Weird didn't even begin to encompass the feelings bubbling up. I put my headphones back on but didn't start any music. I didn't have the energy to actually run back home, so I just walked in silence.

If this was love, love was some bullshit.

The sports banquet was a semiannual affair, held once in the spring and once in the fall. It was a chance for the administration to laud their student-athletes and a chance for us to rub the successes of our respective seasons in each other's faces. Everyone was there: boys' soccer, football, baseball, softball, tennis, volleyball, swim, golf, track & field, cheer.

We entered the converted gym four across and four deep in matching tracksuits; if we were in a musical, we'd be snapping. There was quite a bit of friendly heckling going on before Mr. Caulder—our AP and Athletic Director—took to the podium. London was wriggling his eyebrows and winking at me from the football table. Ugh.

Caulder, a boulder of a man, launched into a stirring speech about the tenacity of athletes, the glory of high school sports, how these were the days of our lives, and so on and so forth. Mr. Davis (our aged principal) spoke next, emphasizing the role of the "student" in student-athlete. He finished his speech with a prayer, a Glory Be To God, and so forth and so on.

Then we got to eat. There was fried chicken, green beans, macaroni and cheese, mashed potatoes, gravy, pasta salad, potato salad, a myriad of casseroles, ROLLS—all the staple food of the South. I loaded my plate to bursting and received an overplucked-eyebrow raise from Joely. I sheepishly put back my third roll.

After the eating was the award-giving-outing. Each coach got the opportunity to get up, talk about their teams, and hand out individual awards. Tasia and I made the All-District Team; Bridget had skipped and thus wasn't around to get noticed during the most crucial game. I could feel Tasia's excitement emanating off her body like heat waves. She even looped her arm through mine as we hip-swished and hair-flipped our way to the podium in order to collect our plaques. I risked a glance back at Bridget to try to gauge her reaction, but she was smiling and cheering just like the rest of the team. It looked genuine.

I couldn't explain what I was feeling.

I was used to her being in the spotlight, collecting accolades—this was something I'd experienced since kindergarten. We had even won this award together last year as sophomores. Maybe it was because, for the first time, she wasn't up there with me that I wasn't basking in reflected limelight.

After the coaches, Mr. Caulder took control of the microphone again and presented awards from the staff: Best Student Worker, Best Role Model, Lives for Jesus, Highest GPA, yada yada yada. Community and academic scholarships were announced for those seniors who had already heard news from colleges. Last—but certainly not least—the coupe de grâce of the night's festivities was the presentation of fall's starting football lineup. The rest of us were jealous, of course, of this obvious display of masculine favoritism, but alas, what were we supposed to do? (Other than date them.)

The boys were paraded up one by one. London was last; the announcement of his succession as starting QB was met with great enthusiasm. There was much grunting and chest-bumping and more than one wistful sigh. Could I blame them? London was a god now, a hometown hero in the making. His jersey stretched taut over his biceps and stomach, jeans slung low on his hips. His hair shone in the halogens, smile genuine and goofy, face touched pink. I should let him go if I had any sense left at all. Let him date a cheerleader, someone who would appreciate him and realize that he was enough. And realize that it was okay to be loved by a cute seventeen-year-old boy. But I was selfish.

The banquet just trickled off after that, with Mr. Caulder wishing us much blood and glory. Joely gathered her girls around a couple tables in the back. She had a plastic bowl, strips of paper, and a pile of pens arrayed on the white tablecloth.

"All right, ladies, you know the drill. Grab a piece of paper and cast your vote for this year's team captain."

We jostled for paper, pens, and writing space. Democracy in action. I sneaked a glance at Bridget; she was unperturbed, a small smile playing on her glossed lips. She never voted for herself—ever. She would never tell me afterward which teammate she'd written down. I scribbled down Bridge's name and tossed my slip into the plastic bowl.

The voting was quick. Joely took the bowl into the hallway to count, and we milled around the table talking about nothing, which was everything in our world.

She reentered the gym, and our babble ceased; Bridget had scooted to the very edge of her chair, ready to spring up when her name was called. Joely had one slip of paper in her hand. "Your new captain for the year is Sophia Salvatore."

It just happened.

The girls were quiet. Joely just grinned expectantly at me and proffered a hand. "Soph, get up here, girl."

I rose slowly, half-expecting someone to yell "Gotcha!" or make some kind of intelligible noise of protest. Joely pulled me into an awkward one-armed hug, the general welcoming home her first lieutenant. There was an outbreak of cheers and clapping but no protesting. I wanted to scream.

I counted the gathered girls quickly—fourteen. We were down one spurned blonde. I had done it. I had unknowingly, unwittingly, usurped the Queen Bee and stolen her crown. And, well, fuck, this was not going to be pretty.

I lay awake in bed long after the banquet had ended, staring at the frilly canopy, a relic from my early years. I had searched for Bridget after the picture-taking and congratulating. No one remarked on her sudden absence, and her car was nowhere to be found.

Joely had even bequeathed the black and white captain's band, which I stuffed unceremoniously into the bottom of my soccer bag. It had been relinquished so freely by Bridget, who'd thought it would be back in her hands within the hour.

I turned the telephone over and over in my hands, toying with the idea of remaining silent, wallowing in my victory, letting her stew.

I dialed her private line—a pink phone kept by her bead. Old habits died hard.

One ring. "Hello?"

"It's me."

"Congratulations."

"It should have been you."

"Don't do that, Soph. You deserve it. Everybody loves you." I listened to her voice, tuned toward any nuance, any hitch of breath, any weepy waver. There was nothing.

"I voted for you," she said.

"Why?"

I could hear her shrug through the line; I could see it too. The delicate lift of her right shoulder—just the one.

"I've always voted for you," she said.

Bridget called me obscenely early Sunday morning, and I barely got out a bleary "Hello" before her hoarse voice cut me through.

"Something's happened."

ELEVEN
March 2006

IT WAS AMAZING HOW one tragedy could fell an entire community. To be honest, JJ Warren did not have much to do with me after I started officially dating London and that news made the rounds at school. His crush faded just as quickly as it had happened. But I felt his loss keenly—after all, he was one of us.

First period was somber. Mr. Davis came over the intercom to announce the loss and inform us that grief counselors would be in the library all day if we needed to talk. I was sure this concession would be abused by some. During the daily moment of prayer, there was complete silence—a phenomenon that hadn't occurred since we'd stopped fearing the wrath of God. The whispering came later. Speculation about what had happened.

There had been a party after the sport's banquet. It stormed that night as well. Rafael—our Raf, Bridget's Raf —was in the passenger seat and walked away with only a scratch. JJ was killed on impact when his car flipped into the ravine. I refused to comment even though everyone knew I had the story first-hand from Bridget.

Each class was the same—quiet but buzzing, solemn eyes, muted laughs, leave if you need to. I ran into Emma in the hallway between third and fourth periods. She was hysterical, hair disheveled, eyes puffy, mascara tracks on her cheeks. I grabbed her and squeezed her as tight as I could, trying to relay comfort through my arms since I had no words for it. She mumbled gibberish into my shoulder.

The bell rang, and still, I held her until she nodded and wiped her face.

My fourth period was Art, which was the saving grace of my day. I was on track to take the Advanced Placement course next year—and so was JJ. Mrs. Pearson already had us brainstorming and sketching for our portfolios.

I arrived late and took my seat, but nobody blinked. Mrs. Pearson was joined at the whiteboard by a slim man in a gray suit. One of the grief counselors, I assumed. He started talking about our loss, the mourning process, what we must be feeling. I zoned out, gaze drifting to JJ's empty seat, two tables over. The kids who used to sit next to him, John

Sperry and Courtney Ellis, had scooted their chairs as far from his as possible while remaining at the same table. Courtney kept eyeing the empty chair as if it were a tangible thing that would reach out and bite her. Or maybe it was a black hole, a desolate expanse of space that would suck them in and destroy their own lives.

The counselor pulled me back when he asked us to get out a blank sheet of paper. I flipped to an empty page in my sketchbook.

"Now, this is a common exercise we use to deal with grief, especially with students who are not sure how to categorize their emotions." He started to work the room, lulling us with his honey-slick voice. "I want you all to write a letter to the deceased. Tell JJ how you feel, recount some good memories, say to him something you never could. Please begin."

Heads bent to the task, and pencils started scratching like we were taking a timed test. I wondered if this was happening in all the classes or just the ones that had JJ. And where would our posthumous letters go?

I started mine with a quick doodle I thought JJ would enjoy: The grief counselor losing his fancy gray pants, emphasizing his snout-ish nose. I wasn't sure how to begin. "Dear," "Hey," "Sup," "Wazzup," "For JJ—with love and squalor"? They all seemed like viable options.

I began with "Dear JJ," even though it sounded corny and forced.

Dear JJ,

I forgive you for calling me beaver-face before I got my braces. I'm sorry I stuck gum on your chair in Mr. Polston's class. I'm sorry I told Shelby you didn't like her when you did because you and Dean were always so annoying. I'm sorry about what London said that day. We could have been friends. You were really talented. I'm sorry Dean and Matt and Rafael will have to suffer through this.

I'm just sorry.

With love & regret,

Sophia

The funeral was on Thursday and was considered an excused absence for everyone wanting to attend.

The church was silent when I entered except for the occasional sniff or blown nose. The doors creaked, the sound reverberating off the fantastically painted high ceilings, and I felt like the saints and angels that populated the stained glass were all staring at me: the latecomer who had almost not shown. I walked up the aisle toward the altar, genuflected, and slid into a pew next to Bridget, who clasped my hand. The church was exploding with people;

almost the entire junior class was there, along with the JV and Varsity basketball teams taking up two whole rows.

His family sat in the front pew. His resplendent, model-esque mom stoically stared straight ahead, and his dad was quietly sobbing, a small pigtailed girl curled in his lap.

I suddenly felt nauseous and hot. I couldn't breathe. It was like all the air had been sucked from the world, leaving only grief and sorrow and futility. I clutched frantically at Bridget's hand as an anchor, and then I bent double and cried.

Father Adrian led the service. Beautiful, unattainable, young. Too young. Far too young to be talking about life and death and JJ's ascent into Heaven. He managed to look serene, solemn, and in complete agony at the same time. Almost like the crucified Jesus that hung above him, eyes thrust Heavenward, resigned to his fate.

I couldn't stand one more minute of the mawkish ceremony. Of the hiccupping ginger two rows back who hadn't spoken to JJ in her life. Of Bridget's sweaty palm stuck so firmly to mine. I lurched out of my seat. I needed air and silence. I was suffocating. Heads turned my way, and mumbles followed my exit as I stumbled down the aisle and out the doors to the parish hall.

I almost ran him over in my haste to find the bathroom.

Rafael was sitting on the steps in the hallway, head on his knees. It looked like I wasn't the only one who couldn't handle the service.

I sat down next to him, pulling my knees to my chest, scraping my chin against my stockings. "Rafael."

He glanced up. "Salvatore." His voice was hoarse, and his eyes were bloodshot and hollow. There was a gouge across his cheek, stitched together and covered in white tape. His navy blazer and khaki pants were wrinkled, and his tie was sloppily knotted. He was haunted and gaunt, and his hands quivered. I had never seen a more broken person. "What are you doing here?"

"Everybody is here."

"No, why are you *here*?"

I knew what he meant: why was I here with him. "Even mortal enemies can sheath the dagger, sometimes." I gave him a small smile.

He stared at me with dead eyes; weariness clung to him like a shadow. "He's dead, Sophia, and I'm not." His gaze went straight through me. "Why didn't I die?"

I was out of my league; I had no answers for him. I was about to offer some platitude right off the back of a How-To Handle Greif pamphlet when Rafael grabbed my hand.

"Sophia." His eyes were wild. "He wasn't drinking."

"I know."

His hand gripped mine so tight I felt my bones grind together.

"No, you don't. He wasn't drinking. Jay didn't have a drop. He is smarter than that." He inhaled sharply. "Was. He was so much smarter than that. He wasn't drinking."

"I know. Rafael, it was an accident."

His grip softened, and his eyes found mine for the first time. They were so wide and green, like a small child discovering something for the first time.

"I swear to God he wasn't drinking."

And then he fell apart. His hacking sobs were unearthly, soul-rending. I had never seen him so vulnerable. I had never known him as anything but an arrogant, womanizing ass. I reached out and ran a hand across his back. He pillowed his head on my shoulder and curled into my body; I wrapped him in both arms, and he cried.

Then there was silence.

A silence so deep and vast it seemed to stretch into forever.

The mystery of our dead letters was solved when they put JJ in the ground.

Someone had collected them—my money was on the snout-nosed grief counselor—in boxes that were upturned over JJ's casket, various scraps of paper sprinkling down like ash. So, it seemed whatever we had said, or left unsaid, would rot and decay along with him.

After the funeral, there was time left to return to school, but most of us decided that we couldn't handle the sad and inquisitive glances of the student body who hadn't attended the funeral.

Shelby, Emma, and I gathered at Bridget's house for the afternoon. Emma and Shelby sat by the stereo, rifling through CDs and murmuring to each other. Bridget stood before a floor-length mirror playing with her hair, and I curled up on the window bench, hot face pressed against the glass.

"I'm thinking about cutting my hair." She had her long ponytail pinned up with pink-tipped fingers. "What do you think?"

There was a chorus of assent from the floor.

"I said, 'What do you think,' Soph?" She was turning her head this way and that, tilting her chin up and down.

I rolled my face toward her, cheeks damp with condensation. "Your face would look fat."

She dropped the ponytail and shot me a venomous, curled-lip glare. "What's your problem?"

"A boy is dead. Nobody gives a fuck about your hair."

There was a stunned silence; I could hear only the nervous clacking of CD cases. Bridget's face was pale but expressionless. Even her lips were pale, devoid of gloss or shine, but her eyes narrowed.

"Yeah, and there's nothing we can do about it. We all liked JJ."

Then she stomped into the bathroom and slammed the door.

Maybe I should have run after her and apologized, but my body refused to move. My encounter with Rafael had stripped me down and left the exposed pieces raw and smarting. Pieces I didn't even know existed. I couldn't handle Bridget's perkiness. And, frankly, I just didn't give a damn about what she thought about me right now.

Shelby was frowning at me. "He was our friend too, Soph."

The death of a peer echoed in mysterious ways. My once laissez-faire mother had become obsessed with the who, when, what, where, and how of all my activities that didn't involve her. She had even finally bought me a cell phone, so there was no excuse for me to not be in contact twenty-four seven. Bridget was overjoyed by my foray into the twenty-first century and her ability to contact me at all times. The little red flip phone in my back pocket buzzed constantly.

Bridget: *where are you*

I was over at London's, sequestered in his bedroom, hiding from Bridget and my parents.

"Take off your clothes," I said.

His eyes lit up, and he grinned, ripping off his shirt. "I like where this is going."

I couldn't help but smile at his enthusiasm. "Homework." I waved my sketchbook. Our latest journal entries for Devotional Studies had asked about future career plans, and I had answered thusly:

I plan to move to New York after I graduate, rent a cheap studio apartment, work a menial job, get high, paint, and basically live a life of sin and depravation.

Sister Constance had been ecstatic to discover that I had a future in mind—any future. She had run straight to Mrs. Pearson with the news. Mrs. Pearson had since been bringing me college brochures, course catalogs, and art books. I had to be great, she said. Not just good, great.

I pulled London's desk chair over to the bed and set my sketchbook up on my crossed knees. London sprawled on the comforter in an exaggerated feminine pose. "Draw me like one of your French boys."

"Stop moving," I chided.

I started with his hands resting on his naked chest. I loved hands and eyes. The minuteness of detail. The expression.

"I still can't believe he's gone," he said, staring contemplatively at the ceiling. "It's weird, you know?"

JJ's death was the only topic people had been talking about for weeks, especially among our class. His memory haunted the cafeteria, library, and locker rooms.

"Question time."

"I'm working," I said, erasing a wonky knuckle.

"What would you do if it was me?"

I imagined he thought it would be beautifully tragic and romantic. Like we were star-crossed lovers or something. I imagined he wanted me to drink the poison.

"It wasn't you."

"It could have been. I was at that party. I could have gotten in JJ's car."

"You wouldn't have. You don't even like them."

"Just answer the question."

I laid the sketchbook down in my lap. "I would wear all black and never love again."

He smiled, but it was sad and quiet. "No, you wouldn't," he said.

Since our first double date had gone so well, Bridget insisted on a second. I think she was really trying to woo Rafael out of the house. He hadn't been at school much in the weeks following JJ's funeral, and when he did show up, he was hollow-eyed and silent and tended to disappear halfway through the day. No one said anything to him, though. What could you say?

We had a mostly uneventful three games of bowling, except for the fact that London found every opportunity possible to put his hands on me. It got so bad that Bridget noticed and gave me a questioning eyebrow raise. If Rafael noticed, he didn't react, which I think made it worse. I felt like a tree getting pissed on.

Then the boys got into an argument about cars or something stupid. Rafael accused London of not knowing how to drive a stick, and London assured Rafael that he did, indeed, know how to drive a stick, and this was somehow Very Important.

So now we were back in the school parking lot, where London was most definitely going to prove he could drive a stick.

Bridget and I were seated on the curb while the boys quibbled by the driver's side of Rafael's sleek and silver car. It looked expensive. My mom would kill me if I let someone else drive my super expensive car. Maybe that's why they were still arguing.

Bridget looped her arm through mine. Her warm body melted softly into mine.

"This is the stupidest shit I've ever seen," she said.

"Agreed."

I was thumbing through my text messages.

Mom: *Let me know if you're spending the night*

Dad: *Curfew is 10*

Glad to know their reconciliation was going so well, and they were on the same page and all that.

I sent *will do* back to Mom and ignored my dad.

Bridget's chin was on my shoulder. "Everything okay?"

I had the urge to shrug, but I didn't want to dislodge her. We hadn't talked much about my dad's reappearance, and I didn't really want to. She'd been through it all with me. Watched the slow and inevitable breakdown of my family. Held me while I sobbed because Dad had come home drunk while she was over, and I had never wanted anyone else to see him like that.

We heard two doors slam and looked up. The boys had finally gotten in the car. London was behind the wheel, Rafael in the passenger seat and looking annoyed even from this distance.

"Well, this should be interesting," I said wryly.

Bridget snorted.

Rafael's car took off with a lot of screeching and sputtering.

"Are you sure you're okay, Soph?"

Ah, and we were back.

"It's just too weird. We've gotten along just fine without him for, like, forever. And he just wants to pretend nothing happened. And everything's the same." Except that wasn't entirely true. Dad wasn't pretending nothing happened; he was pretending that it was just fine because he'd found Jesus again.

There was a tightness in my chest suddenly, and I had to take a deep breath. Bridget's hand found mine and squeezed. I squeezed back, holding on to her for dear life so I wouldn't drown in the feelings trying to bubble to the surface.

"London was weird tonight, yeah?"

A change of subject, bless her. I sniffed and rubbed my nose on my sleeve. "Yeah, he's been acting strange since he said 'I love you.'" And since we'd started having sex.

Her eyebrows shot up. "Really? He said that? Did you say it back?"

"Yeah, sorta."

She frowned. "What's that supposed to mean?"

Telling Bridget that he had basically coerced the admission from me felt too dramatic. I had been a willing participant even though the aftermath had left an uneasy prickling in my limbs. He'd given me an ultimatum, right? Our relationship for three little words.

Before I could answer her, Rafael's car came rolling back in front of us, tires squealing. It bounced like the driver had slammed on the brakes too hard. Both boys got out of the car, not speaking or looking at each other. London's face was red and Rafael had a deep crease between his brows.

Bridget and I stood as one, still holding hands.

London stomped past us. He threw back, "Sophia, let's go."

Excuse me, what? Who did he think he was talking to? "I'm going to stay over at Bridget's, thanks."

He stopped. "You didn't drive."

"Rafael will drop us off."

Rafael had moved closer to us, gaze never leaving London, until we were a weird little sandwich, with me and Bridget in the middle.

I yelped suddenly; London's hand had enclosed my bicep. It didn't hurt, really, but he had startled me with the quick movement.

Rafael was quick, too. One step, and he had shoved London in the chest with a growled, "Don't touch her."

Thankfully, London had released my arm, so I didn't stagger back with him.

He righted quickly and stepped up to Rafael. "You son of a bitch."

"Hey, whoa," I said, throwing both arms out like a damn referee. "You can't fight on school property." I didn't want them to fight anywhere else either, but best take it one step at a time.

"This asshole is trying to get with my girlfriend!" London hollered, red-faced.

"I don't want your damn girlfriend!"

Um, okay, ouch.

"I've seen the way you look at her." London went for my hand again, but I snatched it from his grasp.

"I'm still going over to Bridget's."

I wasn't sure his face could get any redder. He looked like a grape tomato with a flop of blonde hair.

"Are you fucking serious?"

"Yeah, I am. What's your problem?"

That seemed to deflate him for whatever reason. His eyes flicked from me to Bridget to Rafael. Rafael had his hands stuffed in his pockets, casual as you please, except for the murderous eyes and hard slant to his mouth.

London made a sweeping, noncommittal gesture before stomping off to his truck. We just watched him go in silence. The tension in the air was palpable and sticky on my skin, like right before a thunderstorm.

"Hey, who's hungry? Tony's?" I said. Food always made me feel better.

Rafael and Bridget were not looking at me or at each other.

"Yeah, sure," he said, finally.

On the way to Tony's, riding backseat, I got a text from London.

Hey babe, sorry about that stressful day @ practice love you

TWELVE

THE NUMBER THAT SET my phone buzzing wasn't one I recognized. I watched the pixelated digits dance across the LED while I added a flourish to the margins of my homework. My curiosity was thoroughly piqued when the little red phone buzzed again, rotating a fraction of an inch on my desk. I pushed away my lit textbook and thumbed the phone open.

hey

what r u doing

Absolutely titillating.

who's this?

Raf

Well, butter my butt and call me a biscuit.

so, what r u doing?

I raised an eyebrow. The boy was persistent.

I pecked back an answer. *homework*

meet me @ school in 15

It wasn't a question. Or he was just too lazy to add the appropriate punctuation. I had a thousand questions for him, including "Why?" "What do you want?" and "How did you get this number?"

I glanced at the clock: 6:45. Too early for a booty call—as if I would even entertain that idea. What was he up to?

Rafael had been weird since JJ's death. Quiet. Withdrawn. He wandered the hallways alone instead of with his usual entourage. I barely saw him in the cafeteria anymore. Bridget didn't know how to handle this new Raf.

So maybe it was morbid fascination that made me reply, *ok.*

I hastily shoved my homework and textbook into my backpack and discarded the lot on top of my bed. Mom was working late, so Dad was the only gatekeeper left. I could hear him puttering around in the kitchen and the soft drone of the TV. I had taken to parking on the street since there were now two cars in our short driveway. If I was careful, I could get in and out without him noticing. Throwing on my customary athletic jacket, I locked my door and turned the stereo on. Just a low buzz to keep the room from being too quiet and still.

I knocked the screen out of my window, propping it against the house so I could replace it on my return.

Crouching in the damp grass, I listened for any sounds from the house. Anything that would signal my dad's notice of my escape. Hearing nothing, I slunk through the carefully tended bushes to my car.

I found Raf in the faculty parking lot. We had a clear view of the front entrance, but nobody would see us unless they were looking.

He was perched on the trunk of his car, shoes on the expensive bumper. I joined him on the trunk, trying not to leave any scuff marks. Not that his dad couldn't fix it, but my momma had raised me different.

Light spilled from the open front doors, illuminating a milling gaggle of large men in suits and small girls in white, frilly dresses. They looked like dancing cupcakes.

"Did you have one?" Rafael nodded to the crowd filing inside.

It dawned on me suddenly, what was happening at seven on a Friday night.

I laughed. "Me? Pledge my virginity to my father? You know better."

Purity balls were popular among the elementary and middle school moms and dads before their girls succumbed to hot boys and hormones. I couldn't even imagine my mom trying to subject me to such preposterousness. "Sophia, come, let us celebrate your hymen!" Besides, my father had already checked out by my middle school days. Not that I'd appoint him guardian of my virtue anyway.

Raf grinned, and it was the first real emotion I'd seen on his face in weeks besides his incandescent rage at London a few nights ago. "That's right. You gave it up to Hart." He nudged me gently with his elbow; there wasn't any malice in his words, but something churned in my stomach anyway. Why did he care?

"Yep. I'm just a regular old slut."

"Hart doesn't seem like your type."

"And what's my type."

He shrugged.

"Rafael. Are you hitting on me?"

He affected an open-mouthed look of horror.

"Why not?" I huffed.

"You've got a smart mouth."

I nodded sagely. "You prefer sycophants like Bridge."

He leaned onto his elbows and returned his eyes to the doors, now closed. "And you prefer nice boys."

London was supposed to be a nice, decent boy. That's what I kept telling everyone. That's what blonde, blue-eyed, magazine-perfect jawline, All-American quarterbacks were. Right?

"Do you think Father Adrian's in there?" I asked instead.

"Doubt it. He's too progressive for the MAPS." At my puzzled expression, he elaborated, "Mothers Against Premarital Sex."

"You've got to be kidding me."

"Nah. It's a bunch of bored housewives with nothing better to do. My mom's a member." He slid off the trunk, and I got the feeling we were about to arrive at the point of this rendezvous.

I followed him. "She's not doing a very good job."

"Nobody polices dicks."

I expected a grab of the groin to emphasize his statement; that's what the old Raf would have done. New Raf reached into the back seat and pulled out a black duffle bag, his face lighting up with glee when he sat it on the trunk.

"The fuck?"

He glanced at me sidewise. "Don't really know what Hart sees in you."

I resisted the urge to kick him in the shins. "What's in the bag?"

He unzipped it with a flourish and presented the contents to me with his arms spread in a ta-da. There was a small fog machine, a strobe light, and multiple cans of spray paint and silly string.

"Me and Jay were planning this for months," he gibbered excitedly. "We're crashing the party."

Rafael crowed with joy when we found the front doors unlocked. And that's when I heard the sharp *brrrp* of the sirens.

At first, I was petrified, as every normal teenager should be, when ushered into the back of an unmarked police car. But then I realized we hadn't been cuffed, and the lights were off.

"We have rights, you know," I informed the officer.

He adjusted the rearview mirror so his eyes could catch mine. "You're not under arrest." He patted our terribly incriminating goodie bag, which was riding shotgun. "But you were caught red-handed."

"We didn't even *do* anything." Petulance was a strong suit of mine.

Raf's face was split like an overripe peach, grin stretching from ear to ear. He was loving this.

I felt a strange sort of protective loyalty towards him at that moment. He was supposed to do this with JJ. Jay was supposed to be riding with him behind the clean-cut, baby-faced cop, but instead, Raf had chosen me. I had no idea why he would pick me as JJ's replacement, but I sure as hell wasn't going to let him down.

"We're minors. You're not allowed to question us without our parents' consent." I swear I had heard that on some cop TV show. He didn't have to know that I'd rather go to prison than call my parents to come rescue me.

"That's only if you're a suspect," Baby-Face replied.

I was out of clever cop-talk. Slouching in my seat, I leaned in close to Raf and whispered, "What do we do now?"

He shrugged, completely casual and unaffected. His gaze was a million miles away as he watched the streaking of the fluorescent streetlights. "Guess we'll see what happens."

—— *ele* ——

Baby-Face escorted us into the local police station—sans handcuffs—but with a firm grip on both our arms. He seated us in a line of beige plastic bowl chairs outside of what I assumed was his superior's office.

The station was unusually quiet for about eight. The more hardened criminals probably didn't come out until much later. I heard men's laughter from inside the office.

Baby-Face was probably regaling the other officers with a tale about the two delinquents he'd picked up.

There was a groaning of heavy door hinges and the squeaking of shiny boots, and then a different officer stood before us. This one was older, statelier, graying slightly at the temples.

He cast his stern gaze on Rafael and Rafael only.

"Mr. Esparza. Your mother warned us we might be seeing you tonight."

I made a small hissing noise but decided not to interrupt. I would bitch at Raf later for knowing we would get caught.

Raf wasn't looking up but stared intently at his Adidas, one stacked neatly on the other.

"Son," the officer said, much less officially, "this is not the way to go about things." He put a heavily creased hand on Raf's shoulder and took the seat next to him. "This is not the road you want to go down."

Suddenly, I understood.

Suddenly, I felt like an interloper.

The officer knew. Of course he did. We lived in a small town—a town small enough that a mother felt comfortable calling the cops to keep a lookout for her own son.

He might've been at the scene that night.

I squirmed uneasily in my chair. I didn't want to be here with people who had witnessed the aftermath.

"We didn't do anything," Raf repeated the words I'd said in the car, reassuming his usual belligerent swagger.

The officer sighed in a grandfatherly way. As if he'd dealt with this before. As if this was just how things were.

"Vandalism is a crime, Mr. Esparza."

"Good thing we didn't vandalize anything, then."

I wanted to elbow Raf in the ribs. Tell him to shut it before we got arrested for insubordination. Could they arrest you for insubordination?

But the officer was exceedingly patient. "Do you want me to call your father?"

Rafael shook his head, gaze returning to his feet.

"I can call someone," I piped.

The officer nodded and went back into his office, presumably to get me the "authorized" cop phone.

Raf swiveled towards me and almost knocked me from the chair. His face was tight, drawn, and there were splotches of red high on his cheeks.

"Ramsey, he—" Rafael swallowed. "Rode with me in the ambulance. After, you know?"

I could have called anyone else—literally. Shelby, Emma, and even Bridget would have come to our rescue.

So why him?

Father Adrian rolled up to the front of the police station in an old Caddy with a dented fender, a Jesus fish, and a bumper sticker that read "Honk If You Love Jesus."

Rafael's eyebrows shot up so high, I thought they would surely be swallowed by his effortlessly tousled mane.

Father Adrian waved jovially from the front seat, and I grimaced.

Bad move, Sophia, Bad, bad move.

Raf said nothing as we both slid into the backseat like chastised children.

"Not getting into too much trouble, I hope." Father Adrian's eyes met mine in the rearview mirror as his high beams flashed out into the empty street.

"Just a misunderstanding, Father." Rafael squirmed in his seat, deferential to the holy man like he'd been taught.

"Where to, teenage deviants?"

"School." I slumped back in my seat.

"I didn't know you two liked school enough to spend a Friday night there." His mouth quirked adorably.

"It was stupid," Raf muttered.

"I'd like to talk to you on Monday. Okay, Rafael?" He was all sweet concern now.

Raf nodded silently.

A pang of jealousy sliced through my stomach so violently, I thought I would vomit. I sulked in my seat, arms crossed, and glared at the back of Father Adrian's pretty head. He was only doing his job. I'm sure he offered guidance to many a misguided youth.

We rode the rest of the way in silence, only occasionally hearing Father Adrian's voice as he hummed along to some oldies station.

Our cars were the only two left in the parking lot, and Father Adrian sidled up next to mine.

"Thanks, Father," we both said, climbing quickly from the caddy.

"See you at Mass on Sunday." Father Adrian threw the car in reverse.

"Is that a threat?" I chirruped. I couldn't help myself, even knowing Rafael was watching.

"A request." Without a backward glance, he drove off into the night.

Rafael was looking at me with his head cocked; I couldn't interpret his expression. Or I didn't want to.

"That was weird," he said.

I shrugged. There wasn't much I could say to explain anything.

"Hey." He knocked me in the shoulder. "Thanks for, you know, tonight."

I knocked him back. "Stop hitting me."

He looked sheepish, shifting his weight from foot to foot and fiddling his keys. "I didn't mean to get you in trouble."

I scoffed. "That wasn't anything."

He grinned and put his hand back on my shoulder, his touch weirdly gentle, and it was my turn to look sheepish. "I won't tell if you won't."

My heart thudded panicky in my chest. "Tell what?"

"That we're no longer mortal enemies."

THIRTEEN
April 2006

IT IS A TRUTH universally acknowledged that teenage girls in possession of copious amounts of alcohol are in want of a game to embarrass and humiliate their closest friends.

You would think the girl with the alcoholic father would be able to bring the goods, but it had been years since I'd found a stray bottle of vodka behind the cereal and pasta boxes. And now that Dad was firmly aboard the saved and sober train, there wasn't a drop of alcohol to be found. Believe me, I looked in all his old hiding places and came up empty-handed.

So the job fell to the girl with the older brother.

I rolled the bottle around in my hands, and my upper lip curled. "Peach schnapps? Really? This was the best he could do?" My stomach roiled reflexively, watching the clear liquid slosh around the bottle. The rum was already warming my belly.

Emma shrugged. "Beggars can't be choosers."

"This isn't going to end well."

"Oh, just shut it and pour." Bridget wiggled her sticky glass in my face.

I twisted the top, and the plastic made a satisfying cracking sound. The four of us were gathered in Bridget's room again—her's was the only room big enough to disguise our weekend activities—cross-legged in a circle, cups held up in a neat line waiting for a refill.

I poured as neatly as I could, which was a great feat considering we'd already finished a bottle of white rum, my tongue stuck out of the left side of my mouth in concentration.

After the schnapps had been doled out nice and even, Bridget cleared her throat in a very Sister Constance-way. We giggled.

"All right, ladies, here's the name of the game: Truth or Drink." She looked at each of us in turn, making sure to make uncomfortably long eye contact. "Here be the rules. We each take turns asking a question, a truth, and if you choose not to answer your question, you have to take a drink. Capisce?"

Shelby and Emma nodded fervently, eyes big and glassy, but I squirmed and played with the hem of my shorts, fastidiously ignoring the fact that Bridget's eyes were burning a hole in the side of my head.

Bridget waved a lazy hand in Shelby's direction. "Shelbs, why don't you go first?"

Shelby's slender knees were bouncing with excitement; she couldn't taste the danger in the air. She chewed on her bottom lip for a moment, debating her question. "Who do you think is the hottest person at school, Soph?"

I snorted, and white rum threatened to come erupting out of my nostrils. That would burn.

FatherAdrianofcoursehessuchahottie almost came rolling out of my mouth at the same time but drunk me still had enough sense left to know that would burn even more. I was scrambling for a safe answer when Bridget grinned like a Cheshire cat.

"What about your boyfriend?" she purred.

"Oh, yeah. He's hot, but I don't know if he's the hottest."

Emma giggled, sloshing schnapps over her hands.

"What about Matt Arce?" I offered. "I'd say he is definitely the hottest." Matt Arce was a swarthy dreamy senior with dreamy curly hair and sparkly cerulean eyes. No one could deny his general appeal to teenage girls.

Bridget wrinkled her delicate nose. "Acceptable."

"You can't deny my truth!"

"It's your turn."

This time I met the full force of her gaze without flinching. "Have you ever let Raf do...butt stuff to you?"

There was a collective horrified gasp; you would have thought I asked them if he liked to poop on her.

Bridget flipped her loose ponytail—she hadn't cut her hair—and shifted her shoulders like a duck rustling its feathers to shake off excess water.

"I've never let him do anything."

The resounding silence was deafening; Shelby squinted her eyes like she just couldn't see Bridge quite right; Emma's mouth hung open. My face was twisted with consternation.

"What?"

"You heard me." She sounded smug. Like a fat duck settling down proudly over a clutch of eggs.

It made no sense that I, the designated Best Friend, would not know about the state of Bridget's intact hymen. But again, I had not gone running to her when London and I started having sex. I'd gone to Shelby. I trusted her more. But it appeared as if Bridge had gone to no one. We'd all just assumed. Rafael had a reputation. That's what he did.

But maybe it actually made a lot of sense. Maybe that explained their on-again-off-again relationship for the past three years. Bridge wasn't giving it up, so Raf got it somewhere else for a while and then came crawling back. But why? Out of desperation? Some kind of blind hope that the next time, she would be ready to give him a key to the golden temple?

Bridget sat there, a thin purple spaghetti strap slipping off her narrow shoulder. The dewy skin of her chest and neck were flushed splotchy red from the alcohol. Wisps of featherlight hair floated around her head. She looked way young. Maybe she was innocent. But I was having a hard time believing it.

"Why?" I blurted.

"I'm saving myself."

"For Rafael?"

She shrugged. "If he loves me, he'll wait."

My eyebrows scrunched together even harder. From my, granted, limited experience, that seemed like a lot to ask from a horny boy. London glommed onto me every time we were alone—and sometimes in the hallway. I think I had three periods last month just to give myself a break.

And he said he loved me. Ever since that first time.

"So, what do you guys do?" It was a stage-whispered like I just couldn't believe they had anything to talk about.

Shelby was listening with rapt attention, and Emma was chewing her nail with bored indifference, taking covert sips of her drink even though that was against the rules of the game.

"Believe it or not, Sophia, there are other things to do besides have sex." There was something almost malicious about the way she emphasized the word sex. Like she was above it. Like she was suddenly superior to me.

The tiny hairs on the back of my neck prickled at the look in her eyes. I had taken her captain's band, but she could get that back. I was a sullied woman now, something that could never be undone, something that she could hold over me.

I became acutely aware of the way my nails were digging into the palm of my hand and had to consciously relax. She was unruffled. I could be unruffled.

I bared my teeth. "Rafael must really enjoy talking. He talks a lot."

She smiled, and it was feral. I had seen this smile before. When a boy she deemed beneath her dared to ask her out or before a game when she greeted the opposing team. This smile said: *I am going to destroy you. And I am going to love it.*

"I heard that you don't talk very well."

Oh, snap. The bottom fell out of my stomach, taking any color I had in my face with it. And apparently, my capacity for rational thought. Or a sarcastic response. Or any response, really, except for, "What?"

She put the rim of her cup to her glossy lips. "That's what Rafael said. London likes to run his mouth about you. Apparently."

The warmth drained from my extremities, and I suddenly felt stone-cold sober. I felt Shelby's hands on mine —she must've been trying to keep me from spilling my cup—but I knocked her out of the way as I unsteadily gained my feet. I couldn't look at any of them. Pressure was building behind my eyes and up my throat; I was either going to cry or vomit.

"Sophia, don't—"

The rest of Shelby's sentence was cut off by the slamming of the bathroom door. It was the only place close enough for me to take refuge. I heard scuffling and high-pitched girl voices on the other side of the door, but I couldn't make out exactly what they were saying. I pulled my phone from the pocket of my hoodie and shot off a quick text.

pick me up. NOW

Slipping the phone safely back into my pocket, I turned on the faucet and stuck my hands under the blissfully cold water. Bridget's bathroom was a dizzying shade of pink and did nothing to help ease the nausea. Running cold hands down my face did.

The bathroom's décor could have come straight out of the most recent issue of Southern Living except for the creased picture tucked into the frame of the mirror. It was us, back when we were almost the same size before I got broad and she just got tall. Our arms were thrown around each other, cheeks pressed together so tight you could barely make out our eyes.

My skin was hot, and my eyes were bloodshot and swollen; crying would probably be a sweet relief, but I refused to cry here. In her domain. I splashed more water onto my face, trying to scrub away any evidence that I had *feelings*.

There was a quiet tap on the door.

"Babe?"

There was no mistaking the tremor in Bridget's voice. Oh, so now she was apologetic. She only called me "babe" when something had gone very, very wrong.

Not one for waiting, I heard the doorknob jiggle and braced my hands on the porcelain sink. She came in, letting the door click behind her.

"Soph, please." She tugged on the sleeve of my hoodie like a child tugging on their mother's clothes. "Look at me."

I did. Her eyes were so big they swallowed the rest of her features; they were looking at me but not really seeing me.

"I'm so sorry. I didn't mean what I said. I'm so drunk." She hiccupped and clutched harder at my sleeve. "Can you forgive me? Please forgive me, Soph."

"You're such a bitch." I felt emboldened in saying it out loud. She wouldn't remember this tomorrow, anyway. And if she did, it would only be in snippets and fog. She might remember I was mad, but not why. Never why.

"I know. I can be a horrible friend sometimes. I fucked up, and I'm sorry. I'll be better. Promise."

I sighed and pretended I was considering whether or not I was going to absolve her, but we both knew the truth.

"I still love you," I ground out.

If she noticed my tone, it didn't show. She used the hold she already had on my arm to pull me into a crushing—or as much as Bridget could crush me—hug, wrapping her supple arms around my neck and smothering her red face in my hair. My nose pressed into the crook of her neck. She smelled like artificial strawberries and booze.

"You'd have to kill me to make me stop loving you," she breathed into my ear.

My phone vibrated against my belly, and I started, almost catching Bridget with a stray elbow.

I untangled her from around my neck as gently as I could. "My ride's here."

Her face crumbled, and her lips stuck out in a pout of epic proportions. "Please don't leave."

I squeezed her hand on my way out of the bathroom.

Extracting myself from Bridget's house was not a delicate or quick endeavor. The steps proved to be quite difficult to maneuver in my current state, and I got lost in the bowels of the first floor trying to find the back door. Eventually, I just gave up and stumbled out the front.

"What took you so long?" Rafael demanded when I finally managed to pour myself into his passenger seat.

I huffed and puffed, noticeably out of breath from my sprint across the Jameses' front lawn. I needed to stop mixing alcohol and physical exercise.

"I got lost."

He side-eyed me with a cocked eyebrow.

I snuggled into the heated seats, leather squelching against my exposed thighs. "Did you tell Bridget I was bad at the sex?"

Raf was about to put the car in drive but had to stop because he was choking. Then a deep-belly laugh reverberated through the tiny car.

I never noticed how many freckles he had painted across his face; they formed a dark mask in the moonlight from which his eyes glittered.

"Excuse me?"

I heaved an exasperated sigh as if I shouldn't have to explain it to him further. "Bridget said you said London said I was bad at the sex."

He chuckled again. "Yeah, this is probably not the best time to talk about that. And that's not what I said." His fingers brushed my knee as he went for the gear shift. Accident or not, a sizzling warmth zipped up my leg, tore through my belly, and settled in my puffy cheeks. "Let's get you home, drunkie."

My head lolled in his general direction. "I'm not supposed to be home tonight."

Conveniently, Rafael lived in the same sprawling neighborhood as Bridget, so we didn't have far to go. He was the perfect gentleman as he helped me from the car and tucked me into his bed. I had never been inside his room before, but I was too preoccupied by other things to notice much of my surroundings. Except how comfortable his bed was. Except how his smell lingered on the pillows and comforter, so I felt like I was surrounded by evergreens and rippling ponds and other nature crap.

I watched as he grabbed an extra pillow and blanket and curled himself into an overstuffed armchair like a cat.

"You've surprised me, Esparza."

He snorted from his nest. "Were you expecting me to jump your bones at the first available opportunity?"

The comforter I had pulled to my chin rustled with my half-shrug. "You didn't even try to cop a feel."

"You're not my type, Salvatore."

My buzz was starting to fade into a dull ache in my head, but I still had enough liquid courage for one more truth. "Do you love Bridget?"

The silence stretched out so long, I thought he had fallen asleep. Hell, I had almost fallen asleep. His gruff voice roused me.

"I don't think I know what loving her feels like."

"You've changed."

"I lost my best friend. The one person I loved most in the world. The closest thing I had to a brother. I would have died for him. And he's gone. And he's never coming back." I heard the cracking of his voice, how he strained against this heartbreaking confession. The darkness stripped our boundaries down, and sometimes, thoughts slipped out that you don't intend for other people to know. "Bridget just feels irrelevant now."

"I don't love London. He's too good for me." The words coated my tongue, slick like oil.

Rafael snorted.

"What?" I propped myself up on an elbow and had to wait for my head to stop spinning. "What does that mean?"

I looked for his eyes in the dark but couldn't see shit.

"Are you even going to remember this tomorrow?"

"Hell yeah. I didn't drink any tequila."

"That's good to know."

"Spill it." I could feel my eyelids getting heavy and my desire to know Rafael's secret wane. With every passing second, it seemed less and less important.

"London talks about y'alls...exploits in the locker room. I only told Bridget because I thought she would tell you about him saying stuff like that."

I flopped back into the pillows.

Was I supposed to be flattered or upset? Did London tell the other football boys about our tryst in the cab of his truck? Was that supposed to be brag-worthy?

I pulled Rafael's comforter up to my chin, falling into a fitful and tipsy sleep.

FOURTEEN

I WAS STILL SMARTING from Bridget's callous treatment of my delicate ego, but it was chicken nugget day, so that made things better. It also helped that I hadn't seen her all day—she'd been conspicuously absent from Devotional Studies. Sister Constance had greeted her absence with a tight-lipped frown and a disappointing mark in her grade book. Honestly, I was relieved. I didn't have to sit by her and pretend all was forgiven for forty-five minutes.

We were gathered around our table at lunch, and Bridget still had not shown. Emma was on my right, her English textbook open, scrabbling to finish an assignment.

"Jesus, they couldn't write this in English? I get that Shakespeare was some sort of genius or whatever, but I can't understand a word the man's saying." She rubbed furiously at her paper with an eraser.

"It is English," I said, around a mouthful of nugget and mashed potatoes. "Ye olde English."

"I bet Shelby doesn't get it either."

"Naw, it's easy. Just remember everything's either about love, murder, or sex," Shelby said cheerily.

The table guffawed.

Emma stabbed at her book with a highlighter. "You guys are assholes."

And then all fell silent as Bridget James sauntered through the cafeteria, her lunch tray swaying precariously along with her hips.

She took her customary seat at our table without so much as a "hello" and jabbed a straw into her bag of chocolate milk. There were dark circles under her eyes that she had valiantly tried to cover with concealer. Her unnaturally disheveled look was actually quite fetching; she looked ever more like a porcelain doll. I chewed on my bottom lip.

"What do you think about older men?" I asked no one in particular. Anything to diffuse the sudden tension that rose up around the table at her arrival.

"Eww."

"Gross."

"What?"

"Like, relationship-wise?"

Bridget and Shelby shared a look. It was just a brief flickering of the eyes before they both became very interested in their trays.

"I dated a college freshman once," Emma said.

"When?" Bridget looked doubtful.

"A couple summers ago." She closed her book and committed to the conversation. "We hooked up a couple times. They...know how...to do...stuff."

"I don't think that's called dating."

"I think that's called how to catch a predator."

"What kind of stuff?"

"How come we've never heard this before?"

Emma grimaced. "It was only a few times. At work."

"Anyway, I thought you were dating London."

They all turned on me. "I am. We are. It was just a hypothetical question." Bridget and Shelby shared that look again. Emma was obviously out of the loop. "What?" I said.

"Nothing," said Bridget and Shelby in almost perfect unison.

"Obviously not. Spit it out."

"Are you sure you wanna talk about it...here? Now?" said Shelby.

"Talk about what?"

"You know."

"I don't."

"Are you pregnant?" interjected Emma.

"No," I said, although I had no idea where Emma got that notion from any part of our conversation.

"No," Shelby said. I'm glad she was aware of the condition of my eggs as well.

"Then what—"

"Shut it," Bridget said. She glanced around for eavesdroppers and then leaned in close to the table. We leaned over our trays conspiratorially; Emma's tie fell into her mashed potatoes.

Bridget struck me with one of her hollow-eyed stares. "Aimee Reynolds said she saw you eating with a man during Christmas break."

Was she talking about my dad?? Of all people, Bridget should have been able to deduce that if I was eating with an older man, it would have been my damn father. I was staring at the side of her face with what I hoped was a what-the-fuck expression.

"And then." She rapped the table to make sure everyone was paying attention. "Rachel Hughes's dad is a police officer, and she said you got arrested." Her icy gaze cut me through. "With a boy."

Emma's face was dumbfounded, her homework forgotten. Shelby, apparently, had already been informed of my clandestine and possibly disreputable activities. She stoically refused to meet my gaze and was focused instead on a rowdy group of basketball boys a few tables over.

"I didn't get arrested," I mumbled, my nuggets suddenly losing their appeal. Way to be a traitor, Rachel. I thought Art kids were supposed to stick together.

There was a tight feeling blooming in my chest.

I hadn't told anyone about the night with Rafael, and I guess he hadn't either. It felt like something private between us—private, but not wrong. Not scandalous. We hadn't even done anything that would warrant the need to tell. And how come Rachel had my name in her mouth and not Rafael's?

"I think if you're fucking someone else, London has the right to know." Something sparked in her face. Like she knew something I didn't. Like she already knew what the truth was and was hell-bound to make me confess. After he got smart with her that one day we skipped class, I had gotten the impression she didn't care so much for London, so why was she so concerned about my alleged infidelity? Suddenly, it didn't feel like this was about London at all.

"I'm not fucking—" Several people turned in our direction. I lowered my voice. "I'm not fucking anybody. Who are you to lecture me on relationships anyway? You don't know where Rafael is half the time. He's probably groping his way through the basketball team now, and you're too ashamed to even claim him."

I knew I'd just pole-vaulted over the line by Bridget's blank face of disbelief and trembling lip. She probably had not planned on me being so feisty. She slammed her tray against the table before shouldering her book bag and marching off without a backward glance.

"Why'd you have to say something about Rafael?" asked Shelby, her tone implying that she was disappointed in my behavior.

"She started it."

"She was just—"

"I don't remember you defending me Friday night."

She pinked and mumbled to her tray. "I'm tired of watching you two fight."

"She needs to mind her goddamn business."

I left, throwing my lunch, tray and all, into the nearest garbage can.

Figuring I was going to have to be the one to apologize in order to keep the peace, I went in search of Bridget. We still had about ten minutes of lunch left, but she eluded me. I looked in our favorite bathroom, the library, and the locker rooms. The girl moved fast.

London cornered me just as I was approaching her locker. He always seemed to pop up at the most inopportune times.

He gathered me into a hug before I had the chance to turn and run in the opposite direction. "Miss me?"

I wriggled out of his embrace, using my shoulders to bat his grasping arms away.

"What's wrong?"

"I have to go make nice with Bridget." My feet were practically itching to make a quick escape.

"What happened?"

Resisting the urge to huff, I skirted around him. "I don't have time for this," I muttered. He couldn't see my eye roll, but he apparently heard me.

I was halfway down the hall when he yelled, "But you have time for Rafael?"

I screeched to a halt. By this time, the bell for fifth period had rung and kids were meandering their way to class, which meant that the hallway wasn't quite empty. Which meant that people had heard. Which meant that they were forming a circle with the two of us in the center. A sophomore who had stumbled into the center of the newly formed circle was quickly removed by a pair of seniors so that my line of sight to London was unobstructed.

He just stood there with his arms hanging limply down his sides and a dejected look on his face.

I took a couple steps toward him. "We'll talk about this later."

"Am I not enough for you?"

I shuffled closer to him, trying to avoid all the attentive eyes that were trained on our every movement, all the ears hanging on to our every word.

"I don't know what you're talking about."

But a part of me did.

But here was the kicker: how did London know?

"I gave you everything."

"Can you *not* be so dramatic?"

That shut him up.

His face turned a hideous red, and I could see the fury and embarrassment ticking along his jaw.

I regretted the words as soon as they left my mouth, but all I could think was *go away, go away, fix Bridget, fix Bridget.*

I left him standing there basking in humiliation and scurried off, elbowing my way through the crowd. It was hard enough evading their prying eyes; I can't imagine what it would be like trying to avoid what they'll be saying about me tomorrow.

Bridget had either not made it home yet or was ignoring me. Most likely, it was the latter. When she thought I had been sufficiently punished by her silence, she'd call back. Nevertheless, I left an I'm-sorry-please-forgive-me message. I probably should have sent flowers and candy. London was ignoring me as well. All of the remorseful, smooshy text messages sent his way went unanswered. I had sent off messages to Shelby and Raf as well, and only Shelby had replied with a terribly unhelpful frown.

Neither of my parents were home. Mom was at work. Who the hell knew what Dad was up to. I made a mess in the kitchen cooking snacks, watched TV, played Solitaire on the computer, and pretended to be in my room doing homework when Dad did finally make it home. I was lying on my bed, magazine over my face, door closed, but he came in anyway.

"Go do your dishes."

"I didn't do it."

"Who did?"

"Gremlins."

The look on his face was priceless. Like I'd just taken the Lord's name in vain. I bet he wasn't missing me so much anymore. "I'm getting real tired of your attitude. You get in there now and clean up before your mother gets here."

He left the door open. Apparently, that was my signal. Huffing into the kitchen, I made as much noise as one human could possibly make while doing dishes.

It was an awkward couple of hours before Mom got home. And then it got even more awkward because she made me sit in the living room with them and watch the evening news. Halfway through the anchorman's opening monologue, Dad got up with a wheeze and left the room.

I couldn't see him reenter because of my prone position on the couch, but I could hear. I almost died.

"What's this?"

I bolted off the couch and snatched the unused pregnancy test out of his hand. I'd had many a period since becoming a sexually active young adult, so I'd shoved the pregnancy test into a basket under the bathroom sink and forgotten it. I didn't really make much of an effort to hide it, but still, what was he doing rooting around under the sink?

The TV was on mute.

Dad was standing imperiously in the center of the room. "Sophia, explain this."

"Turns out I didn't need it." I headed for my room, the plastic wrapper crinkling in my fisted hand.

"But there was a chance you did?"

"It's none of your business."

"Michael, please."

"No. I have a right to know who my daughter is screwing around with."

"It's none of your fucking business!"

He took a step towards me. I didn't know what he expected me to do, but I decided to hold my ground. I didn't take my eyes off him. We were almost the exact height, so I could stare right into his angry eyes. He let out a frustrated breath. I'm sure this wasn't the family he had expected to come back to.

Mom finally decided to get up and came to stand between us to play mediator. I noticed she was slightly closer to me.

"Michael, that's enough. Both of you." Her head swiveled around, making sure I was included.

"You knew about this?" His breath came out in a gush like he couldn't hold it in anymore.

"London's a nice boy. And she's old enough to make her own decisions." So, Mom had forgotten to mention the fact that I had a boyfriend during one of their many talks.

"Old enough? She's just a child. And you let her go around sinning with every nice boy, like some damn—"

"What? Slut, harlot, tramp, strumpet..."

"Sophia, really. That's no way to talk to your father."

"You're lucky I don't drag you down to confession right now."

I thought of who might be there to hear any confession I might make, someone with a dimpled smile and two crooked teeth. "Do it."

His hands came up in an exasperated gesture. "Don't think I won't, young lady."

"I'll be eighteen in August, thank you. I can fuck anyone I want."

He puffed up, shoulders and chest visibly swelling, like a balloon being filled with hot air. "Not in my house. Not under the Lord's roof!"

I laughed, loud and humorless. "Jesus fucking Christ wouldn't set foot in this house."

I stormed out of the living room and into my bedroom, sticking my desk chair under the doorknob for good measure.

They started yelling. I turned on the radio. I heard Mom's voice above it all, shrill and piercing. It was nice to know she still stood up for something.

You would think that when your life came crumbling down around your ears, there'd be more noise.

That it would sound like something crashing, snapping, breaking—anything but silence. You should be able to hear the destruction.

Silence was the worst.

—elle—

At about midnight, my phone finally buzzed. I was in such a hurry to flip it open, I almost flung it across the room. It was from Rafael.

she saw us

FIFTEEN

I CAME TO DEVOTIONAL Studies the next day, expecting to remain in class for the entire period while dealing with the same frigid reception from Bridget. I found her—looking remarkably cheerier—in deep conversation with Zack and Corion. She was leaning all the way over our table, and there was much whispering and giggling. She glanced up at me when I came in and laughed.

"What?"

"Nothing."

Obviously, it wasn't nothing, or she would not have said nothing. There was something going on. "Bridget. What?"

She slid slowly back into her seat, taking Corion's eyes with her. Zack was looking thoroughly sheepish and uncomfortable, but that was how he always seemed to look. "Zackary," she said, drawing out his name and rolling it around on her tongue, "wanted to know what happened between you and London."

"Oh." Did I even know what had happened between us?

"I said you had your eye on somebody else." She smiled mischievously. Like we were sharing a secret.

"What? I don't...who?"

"Don't play coy, Sophia." She directed her attention back to the boys. Bridget never bothered to keep her voice down, so we had drawn a little circle of interested classmates. "I found this."

With a flourish, she spread a piece of white printer paper out of the desk. Her mortal blow.

I snatched it up before anyone else could and made the mistake of reading the title out loud.

"The 'To Do' List."

Under the title was a neatly typed list of ten names. All boys and all from our class.

It took me and the crowd of onlookers only a second to put two and two together.

"Hey!" Corion snatched the list out of my dumbfounded fingers. "Am I on here?" His dark eyes scanned. "What the fuck, Salvatore? I at least deserve to be on the list."

I didn't pay him much mind because I was too busy staring at Bridget. She stared right back, eyes boring into mine, with her arms crossed.

"That," she said, "is what happened between you and London."

The water bottle was just sitting on the desk, cap abandoned. I don't even know who it belonged to. I snatched it—a move no one was expecting—and dumped it over her head. She was just sitting there with her perfect blonde ponytail, perfect legs, perfect clothes, and perfect life.

For a second, she was eerily still, water rivulets making tracks in her foundation. Hair stuck to the sides of her face. I almost laughed—this was so ridiculous. I could feel the laughter bubbling up.

Then Bridget stood up so fast, she knocked her chair over.

"Girls!" There was a screeching voice. "Girls! Ms. Salvatore, Ms. James. Please collect yourselves," Sister Constance said.

Eyes never leaving my face, Bridget attempted to straighten out her uniform, pulling her cardigan closed to cover a now-damp white polo.

There was something hot and violent about her gaze, the way her eyes narrowed. There was hesitancy there, too, and regret in the set of her shoulders. Like we had come this far, so there was no turning back. We needed to finish our little drama.

Wiping water away on her sleeve, she said, "You nasty slut."

"Bitch."

"Whore."

"Ladies!" Sister Constance's face was a splotchy red, and there were beads of moisture on her forehead. She had probably never seen such a spectacle in all her years of teaching. "Ms. Salvatore, Ms. James, would you please come with me to the principal's office? Do you think you can manage that much?"

The march to the office was a silent one except for the occasional puff of breath from Sister Constance. I could feel Bridget shooting me dirty looks the entire way, but I refused to acknowledge her existence. We were admitted into the presence of the principal without delay, right after the attendance secretary got a glimpse of Bridget's face. Sister Constance manhandled us both into chairs and wasted no time explaining the situation to a startled Mr. Davis, our principal. He was an extremely old man with more wrinkles on his face than skin, more skin on his head than hair, and a pair of bushy white eyebrows. He nodded solemnly while Sister Constance talked and then asked her politely to leave.

Mr. Davis folded his hands across his desk, regarding us through his thick black glasses. "Would someone please explain?" he said.

Bridget launched into a completely ludicrous and well-woven tale where she played the victim, and I was the mindless aggressor.

"Mr. Davis, it's not true." I wasn't even going to try to match Bridget's tale with a story of my own. She could talk her way out of a whale's belly.

"None of it?"

"Well, some of it. I did dump water on her." There was no point in denying that.

He sighed. "May I see the list?"

Oh, shit. The list.

I patted my clothes in a panic, but the damning piece of paper was nowhere to be found on my person. Had Corion kept it?

Bridget just shrugged her shoulders, uncharacteristically unhelpful to an authority figure.

Davis sighed again, heavier this time. "Well, you both know Saint Agnes has a zero-tolerance policy for fighting —"

"It was barely a fight," I interjected.

"Nevertheless," his raspy voice rose over mine, "school policy is school policy. The severity of the altercation will be taken into consideration when deciding on disciplinary action."

I chanced a glance at Bridget. She would not be pleased with whatever disciplinary action Davis decided on.

The tops of her cheeks were tinged pink, arms crossed over her chest. She chewed on her bottom lip, eyes slightly glassy and unfocused.

It was the most I'd ever seen her undone.

In that moment, I itched to reach over the chasm between us and grab her hand, but I quickly stamped the feeling down. It was her fault we landed in Mr. Davis's office about to be punished. What was the point of the list? Was it supposed to be some kind of joke? Were we supposed to be laughing right now instead of on the verge of tears? Is that why she missed class yesterday? Or was it someone else just passing on the message? Pounding started behind my eyes and quickly spread to my temples. I couldn't put the pieces together. I couldn't riddle out how we'd gotten here.

Davis was talking again.

"Go back to class. I'll be in touch with your parents shortly."

Jesus-Dad was going to love this one. Finally, proof that his daughter was the school slut. His worst fears confirmed.

When I was little, I liked to lick seatbelts. Not the actual belts. I would gnaw ceaselessly on the metal buckles. Maybe I had an iron deficiency. No one bothered to ask. My father would smack the belt away. My mother would *tsk tsk* and later try to shame me out of my dirty habit. Now, I felt like that tiny child again, smacked and shamed, only this time it was worse.

We sat around the living room, me in the armchair, my parents on the sofa, a glass of water sweating on the coffee table. The clock ticked. I pulled at a loose string in the upholstery. My mom's eyes were puffy, and her cheeks were red. From embarrassment, I presume. I had just been suspended.

Mom twirled the phone around in her small hands. "That was your principal."

"I know."

"Don't interrupt your mother." Dad squeezed her shoulder.

I slouched back in my chair and turned my attention to worrying a hole in my jeans.

"Mr. Davis said you got in a fight."

I nodded. I figured telling them that it was only a little bit of water and asking why everyone was making it such a big deal was not going to help my case. It didn't matter that there hadn't even been a punch thrown. Davis was going to make an example of us.

"He asked us to come to school for a conference. Said it was important he speak with us." She waited expectantly. "Would you like to explain?"

I could tell the suspense was killing her, but unfortunately, there was nothing I wanted to say.

Mom wrinkled her nose; I wasn't normally so obstinate. Dad leaned over and whispered something in her ear. They started talking as if I was no longer in the room, the conversation revolving around a debate about what to do about me. Words like "grounded" and "punishment" and "take the door off her room" popped up frequently.

What were they going to do to me, really? Take away my car? Then I couldn't go to work. Make me come home straight after school? Then I would miss practice (assuming I still had a spot on the team). Forbid me from seeing my friends? There weren't many of those left.

Nope, I think they were at a loss.

I wondered if Davis had told them the other party was Bridget and what Mom thought of that, considering our history.

I was rapidly losing interest in the whole affair until Mom reached around her back and pulled out a sketchbook—one of MY sketchbooks—that had been wedged in the couch cushions.

I didn't pay it much mind until Mom started flipping through pages. Until I realized that it was the sketchbook I had been using mostly at the beginning of the year when my crush on Father Adrian was still new and shiny and obsessive.

The first page she landed on wasn't so bad. It was just a series of pencil portraits of his face in varying stages of emotions. I had even added hearts-as-eyes to one. Ugh, real mature.

The second page was worse.

Father Adrian's face was imposed on London's naked body and stared damningly up at us all.

I could feel the blood leave my face in a whoosh. I was surprised they couldn't hear it.

Mom was on the edge of her seat, fingertips still attached to the thick cream pages as if she couldn't bear to let it go.

"That's private," I blurted.

She gave me a prickly look. "You left it on your desk."

I felt the sharp, cold knife of betrayal slice through my stomach. Mom had never rummaged through my stuff before. I'm sure the sketchbook wasn't left open to this exact page, waiting to be discovered. So, she had flipped through it. But why?

I wanted to ask *why why why*, but what slipped out was just, "You had no right."

I knew I had immediately made a huge mistake by the way Mom's eyebrows shot up into her hairline and Dad's face turned purple.

"You will show some respect," he huffed, gearing up to say some more, but Mom stalled him with an abruptly raised hand.

"You think I had no right? Do you think I just have a right to go into your room to collect your dirty laundry and leave? Like I'm your maid?"

Her voice was deadly soft and calm. I pressed myself deeper into the cushions of the armchair. Mistake. I had made a mistake. I was no longer dealing with Mom-Mom; Lawyer-Mom had arrived, and how the fuck did I forget my mother was a lawyer?

Time for a subject change.

"It's not even him."

Couldn't they see that? The body obviously belonged to a boy, the lines and planes too soft and round to belong to a fully-grown man. Oddly devoid of hair. There was even a black smudge of charcoal between his legs because I just wasn't ready to immortalize my now ex-boyfriend's junk.

"We'll discuss this more later." She held out her hand, palm up. "Your phone."

Oh, no.

The lump of technology sat cold and heavy in my pocket. Cold and heavy and silent. I had not heard anything from Bridget since The Incident in Devotional Studies. I'd open up our chat, hover over the keyboard, thumbs itching, and then close it again. And again and again.

"Sophia Irene. Your phone. Now."

I slid it from my pocket, laid it in her palm, and watched her fingers close over it.

"We'll revisit your phone privileges after I hear what your principal has to say." She closed the cover of my sketchbook and slid it closer to me across the coffee table. "For now, I'd put that away if you don't want anyone finding it."

I snatched it up and held it close to my chest.

A muscle ticked in Dad's cheek like he was clenching his teeth. Maybe he didn't think losing my phone privileges was enough punishment.

It felt like losing a limb.

If Bridget texted me, I wouldn't be able to respond. She'd think I was deliberately ignoring her. And somehow, that seemed infinitely worse than the mutual stalemate we were engaged in. At least I hoped it was mutual.

Because of our immaculate school records—and a good word from Joely—we only received a one-day suspension. Bridget was going to be SO pissed about it. At least, I was pretty sure she would be if I knew her at all. Since I still hadn't heard anything from her.

My parents' conference with Mr. Davis was conveniently scheduled for the day of my glorious return to school. It was a Friday, so no chapel. Everyone could see my entrance through the front doors, flanked on either side by my sour-faced sentinels. I had dressed for the occasion, hoping for some brownie points. My skirt was pulled down to its proper length, white polo crisp, collar straight and pressed over my green cardigan.

"I'm gonna put my stuff up," I said.

Mom plucked at my sleeve, not wanting to let me out of her sight. Maybe I would disappear. I left them sitting on a bench outside the office, waiting on tenterhooks for the official who would tell them of my crimes. Walking through the hallways, I played a little game I called "Who Knows?" wherein I tried to guess which of my classmates had heard about Sophia Salvatore's sex list and which hadn't...yet. The eyes of my peers that passed over aimlessly were obviously in the dark. A lascivious grin—he knows. An open-mouthed gape—she knows. A stop in tracks and twitter—they know.

WHORE was spray-painted in black across my locker, reaching with drippy fingers to the lockers on either side. It was as good as being branded with a scarlet A like we were still living in the 1800s or some bullshit. We all knew premarital sex was supposed to be a sin, but it didn't feel like a very big one or one we generally gave much thought to. Apparently, someone was thinking about it, though, judging by my vandalized locker. It was one thing to just have sex. It was another to be so public about it, I guess.

"That's mature," I shouted at a group of passing girls— freshmen, I judged, from their terrified expressions and quick scuttle.

I swung back around and was startled by a boy suddenly leaning up against the locker next to mine. He was grinning at me.

"Sophia, right?"

It took me a second to place the square jaw and frosted tips: David Lanasky. Number ten on the list.

"No. Go away. Now. Or I will kick you."

My reputation for fighting must have spread as well because David's anticipatory grin immediately vanished, and he made a hasty exit. Jesus Christ.

I shoved in my backpack, squishing several folders, and slammed the door. The latch clicked with a sort of metallic finality.

My parents were already closeted inside Mr. Davis's office when I returned. The secretary, Mrs. Bogess, waved me back, her expression sad but also a bit curious.

"Ah, Sophia, glad you could join us," Mr. Davis said as I took the last unoccupied chair in front of his desk. Neither of my parents acknowledged my arrival.

"Now, Mr. and Mrs. Salvatore, I've spoken directly with both girls and Sister Constance." He pinched the bridge of his nose, pushing his glasses up. "I'll be speaking with the Jameses as well. I think everyone will agree this seems to be a case of teenage impulsiveness."

"James?" Mom's head snapped to me, carefully managed waves swinging. "Bridget James? You got in a fight with Bridget?"

"It wasn't really a fight," I said quietly.

Davis's gaze slid over to me, and he smiled. It was a tight-lipped smile that broke his face into a labyrinthine maze of wrinkles. I imagined he thought of himself as the kindly old grandpa about to dispense a piece of invaluable wisdom, as grandpas are wont to do. "This is clearly a misguided call for attention. My advice would be to find someone for her to talk to."

"Like a shrink?" Dad spat.

"Maybe a counselor would be best. I know a specialist who deals exclusively with troubled teens."

This felt like the beginning of junior year all over again. Except, instead of sending me to get spiritual guidance from Father Adrian, they were going to send me to get who-knows-what kind of guidance from a professional.

One could only hope they'd be as hot as Father A. Since that went so well last time.

~ele~

After listening to Mr. Davis explain how I needed to keep my nose clean for the rest of the year and my parents huff and sigh, respectively, I was directed to Joely's office in the back of the gym. She had requested to see me.

I was allowed to go by myself since I needed to go to class afterward.

Joely's office was small and stuffed full of old game tapes, clipboards, and coaching books. There was barely enough room on one side of her desk for her to squeeze in and out of the rickety swivel chair. There was a championship banner hanging directly behind her head;

ever since I'd started playing for her, I had wanted my name on that banner. On a new banner.

I couldn't look her in the eye. Couldn't see the disappointment all over her face. Couldn't see the sharp frown.

I stared at my feet. At the cuffed white socks and cleatless Adidas I wore for indoor.

"I'm sorry." My voice was small.

"Sorry doesn't cut it. I've had other parents call me, but I've assured them there's nothing to be concerned about. But I can't have you as captain." Her long acrylics clicked across the top of the desk. "That would be setting a bad example for your teammates. I also reserve the right to cut you from the team for any future infractions, and I better see you at every practice and every conditioning workout, happy and enthusiastic to be there. Is that understood?"

I nodded my head vigorously.

"Good." She slid a piece of paper and pen towards me. It was a variation of our usual contract that we signed at the beginning of each season. I don't think it was legally binding, but it acknowledged our responsibilities as a student and an athlete and was used to fend off indignant parents if their kid got cut or benched for a violation.

Mine had a few amendments, mostly about behavior and using good judgment.

I signed it without hesitation. I would agree to anything Joely asked so long as I got to keep playing.

"Your partner-in-crime was in here this morning, signing her own contract. I trust you two to work out whatever's going on between you before the season starts."

I nodded again. Could we be fixed?

"I promise it won't ever happen again. It was just a... mistake." Was it, though?

Joely stuffed my signed contract into a manila folder. "Everyone makes mistakes, Sophia. It's how you react to those mistakes that matter. Now..." She held out a hand, waiting.

I sat bewildered for a moment, wondering what she wanted, and then I remembered why we were here: she was stripping me of my captainship and wanted the proof.

Sheepishly, I reached into the front pocket of my bag and pulled out the black and white band, CAPTAIN typed out in capital letters across the white space.

As I laid it in her hand, I could have cried. Broken down into tears right then and there and begged her not to take this away from me. But I knew that would be a fruitless endeavor.

Just like Davis, she had examples to make.

SIXTEEN

DR. HOLST WAS THE woman my parents had chosen to shrink my head and figure out what was wrong with me. To see if she could peel away the layers and find the rot underneath.

The good doctor was a slim, prim woman who wore power suits and had three master's degrees—all of which were hanging behind her desk in shiny frames. I guess she was probably trying to convince everyone who came into her office that she was qualified enough to do this job.

It was my third session with Dr. Holst, and today, she had her dark hair in a tight bun and her tortoiseshell glasses perched neatly on the tip of her thin nose. I wanted to mess her up. Ruffle her perfect, straight hair and her perfect, pressed pantsuit.

For my first two meetings, I had refused to say a word. Eventually, Dr. Holst lapsed into silence, and we would just sit and stare at each other. My parents were facilitating this charade, so let them pay top dollar for it.

We both sat in expensive leather armchairs, and Dr. Holst stared at me over the top of her glasses.

I stared defiantly out the window.

It was a gorgeous day, and I resented being cooped up inside on a Saturday instead of being left to my own devices. A soft breeze drifted through a copse of trees, rustling the branches of a white ash.

I figured it was probably time to start talking but Dr. Holst beat me to the punch. "Why don't you tell me about yourself, Sophia?"

"What's there to tell?"

I thought I was pretty standard, really, except for the To-Do List, which wasn't my fault.

"I heard your father left when you were very young, Sophia. How does that make you feel?"

"Don't even. The only issue I have with my dad is that he's a dick."

For once, she stopped looking at me and started scribbling in my file, which was open across her lap.

I imagined her little therapist brain crowing with joy. *Eureka! We have a breakthrough!*

"Why don't you start being honest?"

"You've obviously never met my father."

"You're deflecting."

"You're kind of a bitch." Oops.

I expected anger, fury, frustration, indignation—any variety of affronted emotions, really. But Dr. Holst just smiled and put down her pen.

"Sorry," I mumbled.

"Now you're being honest. Now we can get somewhere."

"But what if I don't want to get anywhere?"

It seemed a pointless exercise anyway. Where could we get? I'd lost my popular boyfriend, my popular best friend, my captainship. I was still allowed to play for my senior year because, as Joely put it, "Maybe now you can concentrate." But she couldn't let me lead anyone. Especially since I'd caused a community-wide scandal. Whether or not Bridget would play was still undecided. I guess I'd find out when summer conditioning practices started at the end of May.

I was a pariah in the town I grew up in. No one talked to me except Rafael and his friends—which didn't do anything to dispel the rumors that I was the school slut. That was the problem with small towns; when you fucked up, everyone found out about it. Which was probably why I had to drive over an hour to see Dr. Holst.

My dad was talking about me in his church group for parents—which he now led. Go figure. And then there was my mom, who had planted herself so very firmly and obviously on my father's side. Her betrayal hurt the most.

ele

There was a surprise waiting for me when I left Dr. Holst's office.

Rafael was in the parking lot, leaning against his fancy car with his hands shoved into the pockets of his supple leather jacket. I tried to ignore the part of my brain making comments about how good he looked scruffy.

"What do you want?" I snapped, trying to breeze past him.

He latched a firm hand onto my arm. "You won't talk to me. I had to ask Shelby where you were."

I gritted my teeth. Damn Shelby and her tender, bleeding heart. "I have nothing to say to you."

"Would you listen for once?"

I swiveled to face him, hiking my crossbody over my head and almost catching him in the swing. "Speak."

A small twitch quirked the corner of his mouth. "I didn't tell Bridget anything. She saw me pick you up that night and then..." He made a weird twirling motion with his hand that I took to symbolize my downward spiral. "You know."

Yes, I knew. Rafael was that kind of boy, and I was that kind of girl—and those kinds of boys and girls do that thing together.

I probably couldn't have saved myself if I tried. Bridget thought she knew us both, but she knew very little.

I hadn't bothered washing, combing, or straightening my hair today, so it poofed out in a wild, frizzy mess. This didn't seem to bother Raf, who wrapped a stray curl around his finger and watched it bounce.

The way he was studying me was strange. Like he'd just discovered something fascinating. His lips were even parted slightly, and I had to ignore the way my stomach flip-flopped. I wanted to jerk away, but I was frozen — watching him watch me.

He let my hair go, and his retreating fingers trailed a hot line down my neck accidentally on purpose. The sneaky bastard.

"I like your hair like this."

"I still hate you."

"This is me flirting with you."

I gaped. "This is *literally* the worst time." I swatted all his appendages away from me. "Are we done?"

"I need you to help me."

We got lost several times among all the other graves in the maze of a cemetery and had to reverse and start over before Rafael finally pulled the car over.

"Do you even know where you're going?"

"Yes. Come on." He got out, and I followed. We only had to pick our way around a couple rows of headstones before we found him.

It was huge, a towering, expensive monument to their love for him. There, engraved in the white marble: John Jackson Warren III.

JJ.

We sat in front of the headstone—a marble slab held aloft by two lithe, winged angels—on a patch of new grass and still fresh earth. Dampness quickly seeped through my jeans.

Rafael pulled my hand into his lap. I let him.

"Nice date spot."

He smiled, and the tension visibly left his body. His shoulders sagged as if relieved that I hadn't fallen to pieces. That I could still find brevity as we sat on our dead peer's grave. His dead best friend and my dead once-almost-paramour.

That's me: nothing is too holy or too sacred.

"I haven't been able to visit him since the funeral." His fingers twitched on mine, palm warm as if it'd been lying in the sun all day. "I wish I could be one of those people."

"What people?"

"Those people who believe everything happens for a reason. That it's all part of some grand plan."

"Are you trying to overshadow my misery?"

"No, I just thought—"

"Thought what? Thought you needed to show me how much worse it could be? That at least she's not dead?" I tried wrenching my hand from his, but he held on tight, squeezing so hard I felt my bones grind together.

"You still lost her. It doesn't matter how."

I seethed, refusing to look at him. Funny how neither of us said a name, but we both knew exactly who we were talking about. She was like a scar that would heal and fade but would never be gone completely.

"Maybe I'm the one who got lost."

I couldn't explain why, so suddenly, I'd harbored so much contempt and envy for her, my best friend. We practically grew up together. Her home was my second home. We had other friends, of course, but it was always just the two of us. Everyone else just revolved in our orbit, drawn by the irresistible gravitational pull of such a pairing. Such fundamentally different girls who had managed to coexist for so long. Maybe we had always been fated to implode.

"Do you think some people are meant to be together?"

I gave him the side-eye of the century. "I'm not one of *those* people."

"I think you are." He smiled, and I swore I could see the sadness, the grief, the guilt that had been haunting his perfect mossy green eyes lift just a little. "Or you wouldn't be here."

"You ambushed me!"

He leaned in closer, and I could smell him. Musky, but not overwhelmingly so. Headier and heavier than the way London had smelled. He always just smelled clean. My heart thudded rapidly and violently against my chest in a way I had never felt before. When he cupped the back of my head, I lost my breath.

I thought: He's going to kiss me.

I thought: This is wrong.

I thought: Maybe not.

I had the thought again that maybe I was broken to feel like this. To want this. But Rafael was broken too—that much I knew.

The damaged could always recognize the damaged, and I saw in him what he saw in me. Sharp little pieces that could cut you to bits, but if you're just strong enough, just tough enough, they can be melded back together.

Not quite the same. Not quite whole. Something else entirely.

But then his hand was on my chin, and his lips met mine, and there was no more room for thoughts.

Rafael's bedroom looked different in the daylight. For one, I could see the abundance of metal band posters that covered every inch of the abhorrent plaid wallpaper. Sprinkled into the décor were the crests of Mexico, Brazil, and the US—his World Cup teams.

He sprawled beside me in the bed, chest heaving, a light sheen of sweat on his brow. "Damn, girl."

My face heated with smug satisfaction. I had worked him over good. If you were going to assume the mantle of town slut, you might as well be good at it.

He caught me staring at one of the many Metallica posters. "'One' is the greatest song by the greatest band there ever was."

I crinkled my nose. "Your taste in music is horrible."

He lifted himself up on an elbow. "Fine. What do you consider to be the greatest song ever?"

"'The Beaches of Cheyenne.' Obviously."

He snorted. "Of course you do. That's such a chick song."

"Well, I'm a chick, so bite me."

"With pleasure." His teeth found my arm, and I squealed.

Desire flooded my body at the same time guilt did; they roiled together in my stomach, making me nauseous. Guilt that I could possibly be enjoying this moment. Guilt that I could be happy after everything that had happened.

Raf's teeth were at my shoulder before I managed to pull away. I cocooned myself in the sheet, still not entirely comfortable with letting all the fleshy bits hang out.

"What?"

"What are we doing?"

"You mean"—he reached under and grabbed the meat of my thigh—"besides this?"

"I'm serious, you tool."

He recoiled. "Oh, so now I'm a tool?"

"That's not what I meant."

"Did it ever once cross your mind that I might actually like you? Smart-mouthed, pissant attitude and all?"

"But why?"

He flopped back down on the bed—rather dramatically, I might add. "Really? We're really going to have this conversation now?"

"We probably should have had it before, but I tend to act before I think." Hence, my current predicament, sitting naked in bed with my ex-best friend's ex-boyfriend. I think. I'm not sure if they ever officially broke up. But I'm sure this was the nail in that coffin.

Raf threw an arm over his eyes. He really did have a banging body. The tendons in his hands and arms stood out whenever he moved, and he was hairier than London. Dusky curls littered his chest and trailed down his abdomen. It was sparse, for now, but I was sure he'd grow into it.

"I feel like I can just be real with you." His eyes were still covered, and he addressed the ceiling. "Like I don't have to pretend to be fine. I can be sad or pissed off or happy, and you won't care."

"It's okay not to be okay with the shit things that happen in your life." I twisted the sheet between restless hands that needed to keep moving. "I hate that my dad left us. I hate that he came back." The words were like vomit; once I started, there was no way to stop them from coming up. Dr. Holst would be so proud. "I hate that my mom let him. I hate that he's all born again and Jesus-fied. I hate that he's trying to fix us. To fix me. I don't need to be fixed."

Rafael uncovered his eyes, and he was frowning, small, delicate lines appearing between his eyebrows. "I'm sorry,

Soph. I didn't know."

Of course he didn't know; no one knew. Except her. The keeper of all my secrets.

SEVENTEEN

April 2006

IT WASN'T EXACTLY PROM.

The school administration believed that there were too many negative connotations on the word "prom"—spiked punch, debauchery on the dance floor, etc.—so we had Spring Formal instead.

I had made up my mind not to go, but Dr. Holst thought it would be good for me. "Stop acting like the town pariah," she said. And then she told my mom. And then my mom got super excited and aggressive about making me go prom dress—oops, Spring Formal dress—shopping.

I had been attempting to give her the silent treatment, much like the one Bridget was giving me, but it was hard. One, because we lived together and she was being obnoxiously nice and making me eat family dinners. And two, she was my mom. My rock. It had just been me and her for so long. My heart hurt. But I was pissed as fuck.

Dad spent a lot of his free time down at the church, which bothered me even more than his presence. It seemed like my alleged antics had caused a rift between them, even though she had taken his side. And that pissed me off even more.

"What about this one?" Mom held up another lurid pink, taffeta dress.

"It's pink. I don't like pink."

She had finally worn me down, and here we were in a specialty dress shop, the T minus 7 hours before Spring Formal was scheduled to start.

Her brow creased. "Most of these are pink."

Most of them were ugly. That was what happened when you have to shop in the big girl rack. They saved all the cute stuff for the size 0, 2, 4, and 6s. Anyone bigger than that gets what's left. Which was mostly pink and horrid.

Mom put the ugly dress back and started rifling through the remaining options, hangers rasping against the metal pole. "You're going to have to pick something. You don't have anything appropriate to wear."

"Maybe I'll just go naked."

"Sophia Irene." The rustling stopped, and I looked up from my phone. She was glaring at me. "I have had enough of this piss-poor, woe-is-me attitude. I know you are unhappy with your father, but we are adults, and it is our relationship, and I don't have to justify that to you. I know it's hard. I *know*. But your father did what he thought was best to get help for himself, and I won't have you hating him because of that."

Her voice had cracked by the end, and I saw her hands trembling.

I had to bite down on my bottom lip to stop myself from bursting into tears. "I don't hate him."

She took a deep breath. "Good. Now, pick a dress."

In the end, we managed to find a big purple one that I thought flattered my shape the best. It was strapless with a beaded bodice and a huge skirt that flared out over my hips. And when I said huge, I mean huge. I felt like a damn Disney princess. But wasn't that the point of these dresses anyway?

She also bought me a pair of strappy silver heels, a big, fake rhinestone necklace, and a beaded clutch that was the same color as my dress.

We held hands in the car on the way home and cried. And then I felt better about a lot of things.

Mom worked on my hair, which mainly involved attacking it with a curling iron. She helped me with my makeup too.

By the end of the prepping and primping process, I was almost feeling excited about going to this thing.

"Do you need me to drop you off?" Mom asked, fluffing my skirt for good measure.

"Shelbs will be here soon."

Rafael had offered to take me to the dance, which was very sweet of him, but I honestly didn't feel like showing up with any boy. I just wanted my friends. Emma wasn't brave enough to choose me over Bridget. Shelby, on the other hand, didn't really care much. High school social status didn't mean much to her, and for that, I was thankful.

Mom kissed me on the cheek, careful to avoid my blush, and ushered me out the door. "Have fun and try not to get suspended again."

"Mom, that's not funny."

"It's a little funny."

The front of Shelby's car was immediately engulfed by the expanse of my skirt. You couldn't see the middle console or the gear shift.

"Could you have possibly picked a bigger dress?"

I tried to gather it all up and keep it on my side, but that was an impossible task. "Probably."

Shelby's dress was teal and slinky, and her long black hair was straight as a poker. It was a little strange to see her so dolled up.

"Girl, you look hot tonight. Expecting to see anyone special?"

She huffed. "Not anyone in this town."

Shelby liked to be punctual, which meant we arrived exactly on time, which meant we were early, and all the cool kids weren't here yet. That honestly suited me just fine because I could post up at a choice table and not have to talk to anyone.

The gym was dark—as if that could disguise the fact that it was still a gym.

Our theme this year was Under the Parisian Sky, so there was a lot of decorative tulle and twinkle lights hanging off every available surface. The tables were draped in dark purple, sprinkled with star confetti, and each had a floating centerpiece.

The only other people here were freshmen—why yes, Spring Formal was an all-ages activity. Shelby went off to talk to some of the JV players, and I immediately made a beeline for the snack table.

I might be cynical about some things—most things—but even I was impressed by the vastness of the snack offerings. I grabbed a plate and started loading up with cheese, little salamis, and crackers.

Mrs. Pearson was manning the punch station—we had four varieties! She ladled out a big glass of peach for me.

"It's good to see you, Sophia."

I saw Mrs. Pearson in class every day, so I'm assuming she meant, "It's good to see you out in public" or "It's good to see you out in public looking normal."

I thanked her for the punch and made my way over to a table as far away from the dance floor as I could get.

It didn't take long for the rest of everyone I didn't want to see to arrive.

London sauntered in with a pack of teammates—who were all dateless, I noticed—but he was quickly accosted by a trio of bleach blond cheerleaders.

Rafael arrived lone-wolf style, looking hot as hell in a completely black tux with an open collar. He acknowledged me with a tilt of his chin.

Bridget was last, Emma trailing in her wake like a forlorn shadow.

I don't know if the whole world stopped spinning for anyone else, but it did for me. I was having trouble breathing.

She was stunning. I might have felt like a Disney princess, but she looked like one. Or one of those old Hollywood actresses, effortlessly elegant and glamorous. Her dress was pale pink, of course, and the skirt swished around her body. She wore pearls—necklace, earrings, hair piece—probably real ones. Her hair was slicked back into a high, tight bun, a few tendrils purposely left free to brush across her face.

Shelby greeted them at the door, and Bridget's face split open in a dazzling grin. She looked happy.

I stuffed a couple pieces of salami into my mouth. I couldn't tell if she asked about me.

The three of them held hands as they twirled out onto the dance floor.

Raf plopped down in a chair next to me and leaned over, kissing the side of my neck. "Wanna dance?"

"No."

"You miss her."

It wasn't a question. He could see what I was staring at so intently. Some rando had his arms wrapped around her waist, face pressed into the back of her head. She was laughing.

"Come on."

He grabbed my arms and tugged me to my feet.

I'll admit that dancing with Raf helped take my mind off a few things. The song currently blasting out over the big speakers was fast and dirty, and Rafael tried his very best to fit our hips together. My ridiculous dress wasn't very conducive to close dancing, although he didn't give up. I wrapped my arms around his neck, and he did just about everything else.

My heart wasn't really all that into dancing, though.

I watched Bridget extricate herself from the erstwhile suitor, miming powdering her nose. I patted Raf on the chest and told him I had to go to the bathroom.

She was already gone by the time I made it out into the fluorescent hallway. "Shit."

"Sophia?" I heard someone slur from behind me.

I cringed and turned around, trying not to totter on my heels.

London was there. The very last person I wanted to see right now, seeing as I had been ignoring his texts.

He staggered a little as he approached. He was missing his jacket and tie, and his crisp white tuxedo shirt was unbuttoned at the top. His skin was flushed and sweaty.

"You've got a lot of nerve, showing up here after what you did."

Um, ouch.

He was still several steps away, but I could smell the vodka wafting off him anyway. It was a familiar, gut-churning stench. Vodka had been one of my dad's favorites.

"I didn't do anything. Not to you, anyway."

I hadn't realized I'd been taking a step back for every step forward he took until my skirt rustled up against a row of lockers.

"You made me look like a wuss. You broke my heart. I was *nice* to you. I did everything right."

His hands tried to grope my shoulders, and I smacked them away.

"Don't touch me."

His hand slammed into the locker. "Did you come here with him? Did you let that Mexican touch you?"

My mouth fell open, momentarily speechless. Rafael might have been an anomaly in our ninety-five percent white school, but I had never heard someone talk about him that way. We grew up together. Good to know alcohol turns grown men into drunks and teenage boys into racist assholes, apparently.

Suddenly London's hands were on me, and his slobbery face was attempting to make contact with mine. My legs might have been restricted by my dress, but that didn't prevent me from driving one of my heels into the top of his foot.

London howled, and I took that opportunity to shove him away. Off-balance, he stumbled, lost his footing, and sprawled out on the tiled floor.

I stomped over to him and bent low. "Rafael is Cuban, asshole. Touch me again and I will end you."

His eyes went wide.

Okay, so that might have been a little dramatic, but I didn't really have a reputation for being levelheaded and calm.

My hands were shaking, and I left him there on the floor.

I needed a drink.

I couldn't find anyone with alcohol, so I went out into the parking lot instead. The brisk air felt good. And then I remembered Shelby had driven, so I couldn't escape. And I had left my clutch inside, so I didn't even have my phone to play Snake while I waited for her to be ready to leave. Worst. Spring Formal. Ever.

I didn't want to go back inside because I didn't want to run into London again. I doubt he would tell anyone what had happened cause then he'd have to admit he'd been felled by a girl. His pride wouldn't be able to handle that.

I just stared at the doors until Raf came out, my beaded clutch in his hands.

He held it out to me. "I told Shelby I was going to take you home."

I slipped the delicate chain over my wrist. "Always coming to my rescue."

"You looked upset."

I shrugged.

He slid an arm around my waist, and I sunk into his familiar, comfortable, vodka-free embrace.

I didn't have the words to tell him what I was feeling. Hell, I didn't even know what I was feeling. Everything felt so off. So wrong. I felt adrift. Like someone had cut my mooring line, and I was floating away from everything and everyone I had previously known. Everything was changing.

He rubbed my back. "Come on, Cinderella. Let's get you home before you turn into a pumpkin."

"Cinderella doesn't turn into a pumpkin. The carriage does."

"There's my little smart-ass."

Despite myself, I grinned.

He grabbed my hand, and we walked together to his car, fingers laced.

"You're a good friend."

"Just a friend, huh?"

"I mean, I'm not ready to date anyone right now. I'm kind of a mess if you couldn't tell."

He twirled me around under his arm, and I let him, enjoying how light he could make my heart feel.

"I'll be anything you need me to be. Deal?"

I stopped twirling and threw my arms around his neck, planting a chaste kiss on his warm lips. "Deal."

EIGHTEEN
May 2006

OFFICIAL CONDITIONING STARTED AT the end of May, only a couple weeks after school ended for the summer.

I made sure I was early, so I was geared up and ready to go by the time everyone else started trickling in. Everyone on the team gave me a wide berth except for Shelby and the gaggle of upcoming freshmen who didn't know any better...yet.

Bridget was last to arrive—right in the middle of Joely's rousing litany of all the running we were going to have to do—and didn't look at me.

My stomach did a weird, crunchy flip-flop.

It was the longest we'd ever gone without speaking. The last time was three days in fourth grade after she'd accidentally broken my favorite butterfly clip. I had a feeling this was significantly worse and wouldn't be mended by a hug and an apology.

Our avoidance of each other was a carefully orchestrated dance.

I ran our preseason mile as fast as I possibly could to stay in front of her.

Joely clicked her stopwatch with raised eyebrows. "You shaved 1.47 off from last season. Impressive, Salvatore."

I gave her a thumbs-up while bending over and pressing my free hand to the stitch in my side. I could feel the pounding of blood through my legs.

When we lined up to do drills, I was on one end of the line, and she was on the other. We knew these drills by heart, by muscle memory. We knew where to stand to not have to face off against each other.

If anyone noticed this delicate avoidance, they didn't say anything.

At least, not until Shelby sidled up to me after practice. "You have to talk to her, you know."

"I know."

She patted my shoulder in a mothering manner and headed off to the parking lot. I knew she meant the gesture in solidarity, but I couldn't help but feel the weight of what I was about to do settle even heavier in my stomach.

I made a big show of helping Joely pack up the equipment and load it into the back of her car, trying to make sure there were few people still around, just in case we were about to make some kind of scene. Joely laid on some more praise about my work ethic today and how she hoped I was able to maintain the same level of focus for the rest of the season, but I was too busy scanning the area for Bridget, hoping she hadn't already left.

She hadn't.

I mumbled something unintelligible at Joely and headed back to the field.

Bridget was on the goal line, juggling her ball. While I was always more interested in power moves, Bridget always was drawn to the tricks.

"Bridge," I squeaked. Then cleared my throat. "Bridget. Can I talk to you?"

She bounced the ball from heel to knee to knee then let it drop, striking it before it could hit the ground. It swished cleanly into the net.

I couldn't help but imagine she wished that ball was my head.

She let her body's momentum swing her to face me, but she still didn't say anything. It was hot and had been a hard practice, so the sweaty tendrils of her ponytail clung to the back of her neck. She still looked unflustered; her narrowed eyes leveled on me.

"Bridget, listen, I, uh...I wanted..." I resisted the urge to shift my weight from foot to foot, acutely aware of my ruddy face and the sweat rolling into my eyes. I pulled on my shorts. "I, uh, just wanted to say that I'm sorry. For everything."

"You dumped water on my head and stole my boyfriend, and that's all you have to say?"

I flapped my arms. "You told everyone I had a sex list! And if I did, none of those boys would have been on it."

The tension seemed to flow out of her, body visibly deflating.

"Can we talk, please?" I asked.

She nodded and sat down on the goal line, stripping her cleats and socks off and sliding her newly freed toes through the grass. I sat down cross-legged beside her, close enough to touch if she reached her hand out.

"I'm sorry," she said. She rubbed her hands down her face. I wasn't accustomed to a fidgety Bridget who was searching for the right words. "I don't know what came over me. It felt like an out-of-body experience, like it wasn't me."

"Don't let Sister Constance hear you say that. She'll want to perform an exorcism."

"It felt like that, a girl possessed. I just..." Her voice trailed off, her gaze wandering off in the distance as well.

"Just what, Bridget?" I said with more force than I meant. I was tired of the silence. Tired of not knowing what the fuck happened. Tired of avoiding each other after almost a decade of basically being merged as one person.

Her blue eyes speared me; they were bright and glassy. "You had London, and then you had Rafael, and then...it felt like there wasn't any room for me anymore. Like, you didn't need me."

I was shocked. Had I become one of those girls? The ones that ditched all their friends when they got a boyfriend? I racked my brain, trying to pinpoint a moment where I had chosen a boy over her but couldn't find much.

A realization dawned. This wasn't about me and London or me and Rafael. It was about me and her.

I knew I was sometimes insecure about losing her; I just never imagined she'd feel the same way. Bridget never appeared insecure about anything.

"Bridgey. I would never ditch you for boys. You're my forever, remember?"

That brought her head up, and she smiled, huge and genuine. How did I ever feel wowed by London's smile when I could bask in this?

"I'm so sorry, Sophia. About the list."

That reminded me. "Where'd it go?"

The list had vanished almost as suddenly as it had appeared. No one ever delivered it to Mr. Davis, and I had hope that the gossip would eventually die down with no concrete evidence. It would become just another Saint Agnes urban legend. It would probably die quicker, though, if Corion would stop airing his grievances about not being included and how could I do that to him.

"I ripped it up into little shreds and set it on fire."

"Did you really?"

"Pissed my mom right off when the smoke alarm started."

I had to hold back a snort at the mental image of prim Mrs. James getting pissed off. "Did you get in a lot of trouble? For, you know, the suspension?"

She shook her head. "They took my phone away." She flipped her sweaty ponytail over her shoulder. "I feel like everyone got a bit draconian about the whole thing. It's not like we punched each other."

"I wouldn't want to damage that pretty face."

"Right," she drawled, unconcerned, face soft and relaxed. "What does Dr. Holst say about the whole thing?"

"You knew?"

She gave me a wry grin. "Shelby told me. I find out everything, Soph, even if you don't wanna tell me. I don't really think you need a therapist, though."

I shrugged. "It's kind of nice to have someone to unload on about my dad. I think I have a lot of unresolved feelings about him leaving."

I was plucking stalks of grass up and making a little pile, but Bridget grabbed my hand, twining her fingers through mine. She didn't have to say anything because she knew. She was there. When I couldn't stand to be in my own house without him, I would go over to hers and cry myself to sleep in her bed. She'd sleep curled against my back like a cat, a warm, solid, familiar presence that made things better for a little while. She never complained, even if it was a school night.

I heaved in a breath, and she squeezed my hand. "You don't have to forgive him all at once, Sophia. But he's still your dad."

I snorted. "Now you sound like Dr. Holst."

"I am exceedingly wise for my age." Another squeeze. "So, are you going to, like, date Rafael?"

There was something in her voice I didn't recognize; it wasn't anger but not exactly curiosity either. And she wasn't looking at me anymore.

I shook my head. "I don't think so. I think we're just better as friends. We've got a lot of combined baggage."

She nodded and didn't say anything else. She fell back onto the grass, and I stretched out to lie beside her. She was tapping a spot on my wrist, almost like a nervous tick.

"What?"

"Nothing."

But the tapping continued.

"Bridget."

She sighed, and I looked over to see her chewing on her bottom lip.

"Just say it. After all this"—I waved my hand in the air as if all the words said between us were still there—"you can tell me anything."

"I have to tell you something," she said like I'd never spoken. She picked over her words like she was reciting rehearsed lines. "I'm going to tell you something, and I want you to know that it doesn't change our friendship or the way I feel about you. I don't want you to think of me any differently, okay?"

I didn't answer, and I don't think she expected me to. I held tighter to her hand, not sure what kind of reveal she was working up to.

"Okay, so, I think I like girls."

I suppose the reveal should have shocked me. But instead of shock, I just felt disgusted with myself. I had been so self-absorbed, I had missed this very important fact about my best friend. How long had she been carrying this around?

"How long have you known?" I looked over again, and this time her eyes were closed, dark lashes fanning slightly pink cheeks.

"Since last summer, I guess, but sometimes it feels like I've always known. I didn't especially like kissing Rafael, but I thought maybe he was just a bad kisser." She pulled a face. "Then, last summer, at church camp, I kissed this girl from Weldon Heights, and it just felt so completely different. She's on the Weldon Heights girls' team; that's why I didn't go to the district game. I couldn't risk having her out me to the team."

"Why didn't you tell me sooner?"

"I wasn't really ready to admit it to myself. And I didn't want anyone on the team to know. I don't want everyone to think I suddenly like them...like that."

"Do you still talk to that girl from Weldon?"

"Sometimes. She's not out at school either, so it's nice to have someone in the same boat as you are. We're not, like, dating or anything."

"Does Rafael know?"

She shrugged, which was an impressive feat considering she was lying flat on her back in the grass. "He never pressured me or anything to have sex. And the 'cheating'"—her air quotes, not mine— "never really bothered me. I mean, it bothered me at first, but then it didn't because he always came back. It was more about how it made me look and not how it made me feel. I don't know. It's complicated."

That, I understood completely.

"Sophia, you can't tell anyone, okay? Not Shelby, not Emma, not Rafael, not anybody. Promise me."

I ran my fingers across my mouth in imitation of a zipper. "Of course. Silent as the grave."

She pushed herself up on one elbow. "No. Promise me." She held her free hand up, fist closed, pinkie out. She wanted me to pinky-swear. We hadn't made a pinky-swear promise since middle school. And I think that pinky-swear was about her having a secret crush on a certain Rafael Esparza.

I wrapped my own pinky around hers, noting the not-so-subtle differences of her slender, perfectly rounded pink nail and my blunt, chewed-to-the-quick one. A habit I couldn't seem to break. "I swear."

Although our reconciliation had gone better than I expected, I still couldn't sleep at night. The thought of kissing Bridget was keeping me wide-awake.

The very idea that I could tangle my fingers in her silky hair and press her lips to mine was maddening. My body tingled in a way I hadn't felt since seeing Brad Pitt's glistening buttocks on the big screen in *Troy*. Or since Rafael. Who I had stopped sleeping with, by the way. I had never experienced the same feeling with London. Yes Rafael, no London, yes Bridget.

I had found myself with a nice conundrum, I suppose.

As with all conundrums, I took my question to the vast knowledge of the internet.

What does it mean when you might like boys and girls?

I found a lot of articles throwing around words like "bisexual," experimenting," and "promiscuous." I didn't even know bisexuality was a thing. And then there were people on the Internet saying it wasn't a thing. It was a phase. They were terribly unhelpful.

My research only led me to analyze almost thirteen years of interactions. Every touch, every glance, every argument, every late-night conversation huddled together in the same bed, breaths mingling, lips close enough to kiss. Every casual "I love you" thrown at each other. Maddening, I tell ya.

I fumbled around in the dark until I found my cell phone stuffed into the pocket of my soccer bag. Since Bridget and I were talking again, she was right there at the top of my messages.

Me: *how did you know?*

Her: *know what?*

Her: *it's 2 AM soph*

I smiled despite myself. It might've been two in the morning, but it took her less than a minute to respond.

Me: *how did you know you wanted to kiss that girl?*

Her: *I don't know. I just did. She was pretty and I wanted to*

Seemed simple enough. My thumbs hovered over the keypad, debating. There were things I wanted to tell her but didn't know if I should. But what if she didn't want to kiss me? We had conditioning tomorrow, and it would be super awkward if she said no, right?

Her: *you have really nice lips*

My stomach clenched.

Me: *oh really? I always thought they were too big for my face*

Her: *no way. They're perfect*

Her: *I bet they're super soft*

Me: *tell me what you'd like to do to them*

And that's how I ended up sexting my best friend.

In the morning, I had to reread my text messages to even believe anything had happened.

Oh, it had happened all right. Even through my sleepless fog, I blushed harder than I've ever blushed before, I'm sure of that.

If I thought our premakeup conditioning practice was awkward as fuck, our postsexting one was even worse.

I didn't know what to say to her in the daylight, and apparently, she felt the same way. Our elaborate avoidance dance continued, except this time, we kept sneaking covert glances at each other. And my heart would jump every time her baby blue's caught mine.

Shelby gave me the funniest look after practice.

"I thought you guys were okay."

I twisted the strap of my bag between sweaty hands. "We are." I think. Maybe. Hell, I didn't even know which way was up anymore.

Shelby looked like she was going to say something else, but Bridget interrupted with an overly cheery, enthusiastic, "Hey, Shelbs!"

She sidled dangerously close to me, the back of her hand brushing mine. My breath hitched.

"Soph and I are going to hang out at my house if you wanna come."

Oh, we were?

I gave Shelby what I hoped was an encouraging smile.

Her eyes flickered between us, a little too suspiciously for my liking. But I couldn't even guess at her thoughts. Could she see the tension radiating between me and Bridget like heat off one-hundred-degree asphalt?

"No, that's okay. I already told my mom I'd help her in the yard today."

"Okay!" Still that high-pitched, affected voice. "We'll see you later, then."

She tugged on my hand and I stopped breathing.

Bridget and I drove separately, so I followed behind her Mustang. The distance and space gave me a little time to gather my thoughts. I knew we were going to talk about what happened last night, and for that, I was glad. After everything that had happened, I didn't want something else left unspoken and festering between us. But was that all we were going to do?

After last night, I was pretty sure Bridget wanted to kiss me too. And I definitely still wanted to kiss her. But I knew in my gut that if we both went there, we'd be moving our relationship into uncharted, unfamiliar territory. And I knew, *I knew*, there would be no going back. I thought I had already lost her once. Was I willing to risk losing her again, possibly forever, if this went horribly horribly wrong?

Bridget's car was parked in the driveway when I pulled up. I checked my phone, and there was already a text from her. Part of me wondered if she was afraid I wouldn't show.

Back doors open

Guess not.

Her parents were not home, which I guess was a blessing in disguise. Since it was the middle of the day on a weekday, they were both at work. We'd taken advantage of this schedule many times over the years to stuff our faces with junk food after practice and watch rated-R movies our parents hadn't given us permission to watch.

I felt a weight press down heavier on my shoulders with each step I took toward Bridget's bedroom. I had felt this kind of nervous trepidation before, right before I took the practical portion of my driver's test, fear of crashing my mom's car almost paralyzing me. I could scarcely remember which switch was the blinker. I remember forgetting to put the car in Park when the sheriff had me practice using the emergency brake. He passed me anyway.

Bridget was standing in the middle of her room when I finally made it up the stairs, re-tying her ponytail. She was barefoot but still in her practice gear: a pair of black Nike shorts and a pink tank top, her purple sports bra clearly peeking through the straps.

She pulled decisively on the ponytail and grinned at me. "Hey."

I knew it was now or never. Grow a pair, Sophia.

I barely registered the muffled sound of my keys and phone hitting the carpet, and I crossed the space between us with quick steps.

Our faces crashed together, and I felt her smile against my lips.

NINETEEN

WE EVENTUALLY MADE IT to the bed, only losing our shirts along the way, between furious kisses. It was like once we started, there was no way in hell we would be stopped.

I was on my back, and she straddled my hips, looking down at me with a flushed, sweaty face.

Kissing her was different than kissing boys. Not bad, not better, just different. Softer, sweeter, more pliant, maybe. She tasted like strawberry lip gloss.

I ran my hands over the planes of her flat stomach, over the soft ridges of her abdominal muscles. She had the beginnings of a baby six-pack.

She laced her fingers through mine and pushed my hands back, leaning down to bite at my bottom lip. The nip was surprising, and I gasped. I felt her warm breath across my neck as she laughed. She released my hands and sat back, tracing whorls into my exposed stomach. My breath hitched at every soft brush of her fingers. I clenched my fingers into the taut muscles of her smooth thighs.

"What are you thinking?"

What was I thinking? That we were out of our minds. That there was no way our friends were going to understand this—us. That this, and us, felt insanely good. That I didn't want her to stop.

"I'm thinking you've done this before." Her hands were so sure, so confident.

She laughed again, and it was low and sultry, a sound I'd never heard her make before. "I haven't, actually." Her fingers skimmed the waistband of my shorts. "At least, not all the way."

She leaned down to kiss me again, and it was my turn to catch her lips with my teeth, thoroughly enjoying the sound she made. I pressed her body tighter to mine, and her hand dipped into my shorts. My hips bucked against hers.

"I'm also thinking we both need showers." It was a breathless, half-formed thought. Like I'd really give up the sensation of her hot, sweaty skin against mine.

She pressed down with two fingers. "We can shower later."

—— *ell* ——

We did end up showering later.

It was quite a feat of athleticism to get us both showered, two manes of hair rinsed and shampooed, all the while continuing to touch each other.

We sprawled out on the bed after, hair still damp from the shower. Bridget had naturally straight hair, but when she let it air-dry, the shorter baby hairs around her neck and face shrunk up into golden ringlets. It was pretty adorable.

"Don't move," I said.

Ever since The Incident, I had taken to carrying my sketchbook around with me everywhere to keep it away from prying eyes. I retrieved my sketchbook from my discarded soccer bag along with a truncated pencil. It was all I had, so it would have to do.

Bridget had followed my instructions.

When I flopped back on the bed and flipped to a fresh, crisp page, she smiled, lazy and indulgent.

I repositioned her limp arms, so one lay across her chest and the other above her head. I started by blocking out where her eyes, nose, and mouth would go.

"This is the first time you've drawn me."

"Yeah, well, I need the practice. I think I want to do portraits for my portfolio next year." I added her oval face and the cuts of her sharp jaw.

"You're really talented, you know."

"You usually just scold me for the work I do for Sister Constance."

"Well, you never show me any of your real stuff."

I focused on filling in her eyelashes and the shadows around her lips. "So what happens now?"

I could tell she wanted to shrug by the way her arms tensed up, but like a true muse, she remained perfectly still. "Whatever you want to happen."

I used my middle finger to smudge in the suggestion of hair. "I mean, I'm okay with what we are."

She nodded like she knew exactly what I was talking about, even if I wasn't sure what I was talking about. I guess we would figure it out along the way.

I finished my quick sketch and held it up for her to see. It was far from perfect, and I could definitely do her better justice with a set of charcoals, but she seemed pleased.

She smiled. "Is that really what I look like?"

I looked back at the page. "Uh, yeah."

"I'm very...delicate."

"You're quite birdlike."

She nudged me in the side with her knee. "I could still outmaneuver you any time, any place."

"Not if I just knocked you over, baby bird."

She moved like lightning, and in a moment, she was on top of me, trying to steamroll over me. It was something we used to do at sleepovers in middle school. There were usually more people, though. Since it was only me, she ended up just splayed across my back, steamroller-less.

"Hey, I have a serious question for you."

"Oh yeah?"

She rolled off my back and settled beside me on the bed, legs draped over mine. I enjoyed the weight and warmth of her legs. I reached out and threaded my fingers through hers.

I felt content in my heart, but the significance of what we'd done—twice—settled like a stone in my belly.

"What would Sister Constance think?" It was more a question for myself, but Bridget's head whipped in my direction.

"Does it matter?"

I squeezed her hand. "No, but..."

I let the sentence hang there between us. She knew what it meant. All the Sunday school classes we went to. All our years at Catholic school. Kids didn't come out at our school. Kids came out after they graduated and then were whispered about by the remaining student body like an urban legend.

"But," she picked up, "why would I keep covenant with a church that hates me?"

I was no poster child for Catholicism, but it surprised me how easily Bridget seemed to let the church go. Bridget was a capital G Good Girl. At least, that's what it looked like. She followed all the rules, toed all the lines, dotted all her Is and crossed all her Ts. I was supposed to be the one in rebellion.

"So, you don't believe in God?"

"I didn't say that. I believe you can have faith without some dude in a white dress telling you what to do."

"I'm pretty sure it's illegal to talk about the Pope that way."

"The Pope is not God, and the church is not God, and Sister Constance is not God."

"When did you get so smart?"

She grinned. "I've been thinking about this for a while."

I leaned over and planted a kiss on her forehead.

I was in need of some spiritual guidance, stat. I wasn't sure how to get in contact with the expert outside of the school year, and I didn't want to approach him at church because

I didn't want my parents to see. Or anyone else, for that matter.

After the discovery of my illicit drawing, I especially didn't want my parents to see and make any weird assumptions.

It was actually absurdly easy.

All I had to do was look him up on the archdiocese website, and I found his parish contact info.

I composed the most innocuous email I could think of. I simply said I was struggling with a spiritual dilemma and needed his guidance...which was one hundred percent true.

It took him a week to respond, but finally, soccersprite18@hotmail.com received her reply from fatherab@stagnes.com.

I probably could have guessed that, but whatever.

He said he'd be happy to help and to meet him at a coffee shop two counties over this Saturday at ten. I'd have to miss a conditioning workout, but I felt like I'd rebuilt enough credit with Joely that she'd let the practice slide. I'd just tell her one of my hammies was sore, and I wanted to lay it up for a day or two. She took injuries seriously.

The day of our meeting, I put on my usual summer uniform—T-shirt and shorts, hair pulled back in a fuzzy ponytail. Old Sophia might have taken this opportunity to gussy up a little bit, but new Sophia was on the sort of straight and narrow.

Father Adrian beat me to the coffee shop and was sitting at a small table, reading. If he noticed me come in, he didn't react, so I went up to the counter and ordered the kind of drink that would have made Joely red with indignation.

I held the frothy confection out in front of me with both hands like a shield as I approached his table.

"Uh, hi."

He raised his head and smiled warmly. I could feel the heat immediately flood my face. Jesus Christ, I was incorrigible.

He closed his book and set it neatly on the table. "Sit, Sophia."

I practically fell into the empty chair. It was time to make small talk, but I was horrible at that anyway, so I tried to look anywhere except at his perfect face. He had cut his hair; it was almost military-short, which was another good look on him. His thick, black-framed glasses made him look like a hot nerd.

"You said you had a spiritual dilemma?"

I was glad someone could keep their wits about them. "Uh, yeah. I thought you might be able to, uh, help."

"Helping people with their spiritual dilemmas is my specialty." He smiled again. His teeth weren't showing, but still. Ugh. He must have read the indecision on my face because he said, "Do you want to talk about something else first?"

He peered at me over the tops of his glasses, and I felt very much like I was back in Dr. Holst's office. He seemed to be employing the same kind of tricks she did, which I suppose wasn't surprising. They were in the same kind of business of trying to get people to spill their deepest, darkest secrets, after all.

I didn't come all the way out here to talk about something else, so I figured it would just be best to just get it over with. I took a sip of my flavored coffee for courage. "Okay, about my dilemma."

He sat up a little straighter in his chair. "I'm all ears."

I tried to think of a delicate way of putting it, but was there a clever euphemism for "I'm sleeping with a girl, so not only am I having premarital sex, I'm having premarital sex with a chick"? I guess I could just tell him I was gay, but that didn't feel right. Lesbian didn't quite fit either because then why was the hot priest still giving me the warm fuzzies? I just felt like I was still being me.

"Sophia? Are you okay?"

I realized I had let the silence sit for an uncomfortably long time, and I was chewing on my bottom lip. "Look." I stuck my finger in his direction like I was about to give a mom-lecture. "I like boys...and apparently girls too. And I know that's supposed to be bad. 'If a man lies with a man as with a woman, both of them have committed an abomination; they shall surely be put to death; their blood is upon them.' I'm assuming that works both ways. But it doesn't feel bad, and I don't know what to do."

His brow furrowed. "'There is only one Lawgiver and Judge, the one who is able to save and destroy. But you... who are you to judge your neighbor?'"

"'You shall not lie with a man as with a woman; it is an abomination.'"

"Stop quoting Leviticus at me. I hate that book." He said it with a vehemence that I hadn't experienced with him before. Father Adrian could usually be counted on to be cool, calm, and collected.

I shrugged. I was out of Bible quotes anyway.

"Sophia, God didn't write the Bible. Men did. And, as I'm sure you know, man is not infallible."

I could think of several men—and boys—I knew who would fit that bill. Nobody was perfect, I knew that, but this wasn't about being perfect. This was about being damned.

"Do you think I'm going to Hell for liking a girl?"

"Do you think you're going to Hell for liking a girl?" he asked. "Do you think God sends people to Hell because they happen to love differently? 'Let no debt remain outstanding, except the continuing debt to love one another, for whoever loves others has fulfilled the law.'"

"I think God probably has bigger fish to fry," I mumbled, poking at my drink with the straw. Did I really think I was an abomination? Did I really believe anything I had parroted at Father Adrian? And what about that sexy Song of Solomon interlude, huh? They just throw that in there and then tell us we're supposed to be chaste and pure and all that shit? Seemed kind of contradictory.

"Listen, Sophia, I could sit here all day quoting scripture and debating theology with you. But nobody can tell you how to think or feel about your sexuality or religious beliefs. Those are conclusions you have to draw for yourself." His head was tilted slightly to the left, and he had this soft, hopeful, encouraging look on his face. Like telling me I had to think for myself was somehow an earth-shattering realization.

"Well, you're about as helpful as the people on the Internet." Which is to say, not much.

"You know my opinion, which is usually in contrast to that of my peers anyway. What you do with it is up to you.

We're all sinners."

If God could forgive an alcoholic father who abandoned his family, He was just going to have to forgive me, too.

TWENTY

BRIDGET WAS GETTING HER hair cut.

I leaned closer to the mirror to examine the red swathes left behind on my eyebrows and upper lip by the wax. It was a good thing we had a few weeks before senior year started so my skin could return to a more normal color.

"Do you think anyone will notice?"

I raised my newly immaculate brows.

The stylist was fluffing Bridget's obviously shorter, very noticeable hairdo. The famous silky ponytail was gone, replaced by an edgy bob that framed her face. It was the kind of style I'd want if my hair wasn't just a giant fluff ball.

"I think people will notice."

Bridget worried at her bottom lip.

"You look great, honey," the stylist said. "Going to drive the boys crazy this year."

Bridget's eyes caught mine in the mirror, and I felt the rest of my face go as red as my abused eyebrows. Her cheeks just pinked adorably because she was adorable.

"Anyway," I said, probably too loudly. We were still dancing around public displays of affection in front of other people. "I have to go. Rafael is waiting."

"Sure. I'll see you later."

She winked at me while the stylist ran a straight iron over her new front pieces, oblivious.

"So, you're telling me both of my ex-girlfriends are dating... each other?"

"Technically, we never dated."

"Technically."

Rafael's expression was something I could only describe as polite befuddlement, like he was trying very hard to not make any expression at all. The tone of his voice was the same.

We sat on barstools around his kitchen island. Both his parents were working, and his abuela was at church for a meeting with her knitting club. There was an assortment of chips and dips on the island for whatever suited your mood—tortilla chips and his dad's homemade salsa, regular potato chips and sour cream dip. There was also cold pizza and tamales available. Rafael sure knew his way around a girl's heart.

He carefully arranged banana peppers on his slice of reheated pepperoni.

"How long?"

"How long what?"

His mouth quirked. "Are you being deliberately thick? That's unlike you."

It finally dawned on me that this might be hard for him. He and Bridget had been an item for years, and while he probably never loved me, he might have loved her. Or thought he did. You can't spend that much time with someone and not care about them. Bridget and I had both agreed that if anyone should know about us, it should be him.

"Not long. It happened after we stopped hooking up." I took a chip and loaded it up with salsa just to have something to do with my hands.

Rafael continued to pile the banana peppers onto his slice until you almost couldn't recognize it as pizza anymore, and I had a feeling he was just stalling for time.

"Did you know? Or, er, guess? About Bridget?" I asked.

He shook his head. "Not really. I mean, it makes sense in a way." He scooped a bite into his mouth and chewed contemplatively. "We never had sex, as I'm sure you already know. She shut that down right quick." He smiled down at his plate as if he was remembering a fond memory. I wondered what the memory looked like. If he had made his first move in his car, or hers, or his bedroom, surrounded by familiar things. I wracked my brain, trying to remember if she had told me. But she had always kept the interworking of her relationship with Rafael close. "I always thought it was a Catholic thing. And I never initiated again after that one time. I always waited for her, and then she never did."

"You're like Shrek. The layers just keep peeling away."

He chucked a pepper at my face. "Shut up."

"I mean it! I always just assumed you were a regular horndog. You're, like, a noble horndog."

He grinned finally, that knee-weakening, stomach-fluttering, bad boy grin that split his whole face. "Yeah, well." A frown now. "I thought me and you, you know, had something."

Oh no. I felt the panic rise up my throat. Was this a breakup conversation? Were we having a breakup conversation and I didn't know it? Did he want some kind of closure? I thought back to the beginning of junior year and the list I'd made. Get boyfriend. Now I'd cycled through two boyfriends (apparently) and was on my first girlfriend. It was almost too much for my tiny teenage brain to handle.

"Uh," I started unhelpfully. How was I supposed to explain Bridget and our history? I'm sure it only made sense to us and looked like a train wreck of emotions and hormones to outsiders. "Uh, I think we did for a while. I definitely still care about you. And I know Bridget does too. It's just...me and her are..." I threw my hands together in the imitation of an explosion.

That seemed to satisfy him for the moment; he moved on to a tamale. "So, are you going to tell anyone else?"

"We haven't talked about that yet. I kinda want to tell my mom."

"I wouldn't."

"Why not?"

"Because. It's your senior year. You're at the top of the social food chain. Why ruin a good thing?"

I honestly hadn't thought that far ahead yet; Bridget and I were just getting the hang of this new shift in our relationship. But the thought of being each other's dirty little secrets for a whole year felt...well, dirty. It made me squirm in my chair. I didn't want to think of us as dirty, and I was sure Bridget didn't either.

"Listen, my mom's white, my dad has two degrees, and I've never been to Cuba. I got a B in Spanish, for fuck's sake. I don't play soccer at school because I refuse to become some Latino cliché. It doesn't matter. They latch on to whatever's different and never let you forget it."

"Not everyone is like that." It sounded naïve even as the words left my mouth. Of course, I wouldn't know what Rafael experienced. I wasn't around twenty-four seven. I remembered London at Spring Formal. His feelings were always there, bubbling under the sweet veneer of his blonde
hair and blue eyes.

"A lot of people are like that, Sophia. You just haven't experienced it yet."

I hopped down off my chair and went to wrap my arms around his back, cheek to the back of his head. I sniffed. "You smell great."

He snorted. "Way to change the subject."

"I'll think about it, I promise. I have to talk to Bridget. It's not just about me."

"Well, that's new coming from you."

I squeezed him a little tighter. "Not fair." He sighed, and I felt his chest expand, and then he laid his warm hand over mine. "I'm sorry, Rafael. I really am. I can't lose you, not after just getting her back."

"I said I'd be anything you needed, remember?"

When I got home, the house was dark. I flipped on the kitchen light and screamed.

"Jesus Christ, that's creepy as fuck."

Dad was seated at the kitchen table, in the damn dark, a hand on a bottle of top shelf bourbon on the table in front of him. The use of the Lord's name in vain and profanity hadn't stirred him. He was staring at the amber liquid, fingers tracing the label.

"Dad?"

His fingers drifted higher to the signature logo embossed on the glass. It was a gesture I recognized. Dad used to love celebrating with expensive bourbon, and so he'd celebrate a whole damn lot. Whenever he went to pour a glass, he'd rub the pad of his thumb over the logo, almost reverently.

"You know," he said, "I haven't even looked at a bottle of alcohol in three years."

I shuffled farther into the kitchen, moving slowly as if he'd startle. "Why now?"

"It was a gift. From the parish council. For my service."

Go figure. A bunch of uppity women who knew nothing about our lives gave my recovering alcoholic father a bottle of bourbon.

I made a quick decision. Lunging forward, I grabbed the bottle right around the neck. If Dad couldn't say no, I'd do it for him.

His eyes went wide, but there was otherwise no movement. I popped the cap and upended the bottle over the sink. He watched me, watched the amber liquid cascade out. The smell drifted up, pungent and sweet.

When it was all gone, I heard him sigh. I turned the water on to wash away the smell.

"There." The bottle clinked against the counter. "All gone."

He rubbed his face. There's a ring of dark stubble. "I'm trying so hard. This is so hard."

Old Sophia would have made some smart-ass comment and fled from the room. Fled from his confession. But I was new, don't-be-an-asshole, Sophia. I could feel my phone vibrating in my back pocket—probably Bridget, calling to get an update on how everything went with Rafael.

I slid the phone from my pocket so I wouldn't squish it and sat down. Another stop on my apology tour, except I wasn't sure how this conversation was supposed to go. I didn't feel particularly apologetic towards him.

His eyes were red, and the skin around them swollen. If I didn't know any better, I'd swear he'd been drinking again.

"I want to apologize." He rubbed his hands on his jeans. "I don't think showing your sketchbook to your mom was my best parenting decision."

He'd made better parenting decisions? I bit my tongue.

Wait, what?

That conversation had definitely gone the other way, and they had definitely let me think Mom had found it. She had taken the blame; shielded him from my ire. I guess it made sense, in a way. She always was the authority figure in our house. That was a responsibility Drunk-Dad didn't have much patience for.

"You grew up while I was gone, and I didn't know how to deal with the pregnancy test and the suspension and the fact that my little girl likes boys."

I bit my tongue again. This didn't feel like the most opportune time to burst that particular bubble.

"I don't know who you are anymore. When I left, you were still collecting fairy statues and rocks, and now...I don't know. I was just looking for a clue."

He was looking at me expectantly. It was apparently my turn.

Dr. Holst was helping me unpack how I felt about my father. Helping me understand that you can love and need someone and not particularly like them or agree with their decisions.

"I needed you."

I felt the tightness in my chest that was the harbinger of tears. No no no no no. Dad could tell they were coming too because his whole face creased with concern. I crossed my arms over my chest and held on to my shoulders, hoping the movement would keep some of the emotion caged inside.

It didn't work.

Dad was up from his chair in a heartbeat and wrapping his arms around only the top half of my body since I was still seated. It was the most awkward hug in the history of hugs. My arms and face were trapped against his sternum. He smelled like I always remembered him smelling. Woodsy.

I did what I could to wipe my eyes and wondered how long this hug was going to last.

"Dad, I can't breathe."

He let out what I could only describe as a chortle and released me with a pat between my shoulder blades.

"Sorry, hun." He stuck his hands in his pockets and started shuffling his feet, which were gestures I would expect from boys but not from a man nearing fifty. At least I thought he was almost fifty. "You know I love you, right?"

"Yeah, Dad, I know."

TWENTY-ONE

August 2006

THE WEEKEND BEFORE THE first day of school, the PTA and athletic boosters always hosted a back-to-school bonfire for the whole school. They set the bonfire up in the large expanse of empty field that bordered the football field. I'm not sure why we had a large random field; I had heard rumors that it was being saved for a new baseball set-up, but the money had yet to come through. They turned the spotlights on and opened the concession stand —which was my favorite part. I had a wad of dollar bills stuffed in the pocket of my jeans for snacks.

Bridget picked me up, and we held hands until we got to school.

It was always interesting to see everyone outside in their civilian clothes. We were used to a variety of uniforms: academic and athletic and casual weekend wear. Which, for me, was usually sweats or Nike shorts and T-shirts. I dressed up a little for the occasion and wore my least frayed flare jeans, a plain, black tee, my fuchsia Converse, and several studded belts for pizzazz. Bridget had on a denim mini skirt with a purposely frayed hem, flip-flops, and two layered polos. Her new bob floated around her face effortlessly.

I followed Bridget and her thwacking flip-flops through the parking lot. Emma and Shelby were waiting for us by the concession booth. Shelby had an armful of foil-wrapped hot dogs, and Emma eyed me suspiciously, keeping distance between us as if my reputation was contagious.

I don't think she had fully accepted the melding of our foursome again—not when so recently it had just been her and Bridget.

Bridget's arm brushed mine in a way that made my toes tingle. I itched to grab her hand but knew I couldn't. Not in front of all these witnesses.

Shelby handed me a hot dog and some ketchup packets.

"London here?" I cradled my dog carefully and ripped a packet with my teeth.

Shelby glanced around. "Haven't seen him yet." She tossed her head in the direction of the field. "All the football players are over there."

I'd seen London in the hallways at school but hadn't spoken to him since Spring Formal. He'd made no moves to talk to me either, which was a good decision on his part. I'd hate to have to ruin his sparkling reputation his senior year by starting the completely true rumor that he'd been bested by a girl. I'd only gotten the occasional nasty text from an unknown number, but I chose to attribute those to the sex list debacle. Not that I'd put it past London to casually let my number slip out of spite.

The football team was on the field, doing a shirts versus practice jerseys scrimmage. Since we were a good Catholic school, there were never any skins.

Emma eyed the field with interest. "Let's go watch." She wore a tight Happy Bunny tee, matching blue-checked shorts, and platform sandals. Her long legs were brown and shiny like she'd been extra generous with the self-tanner.

Bridget shrugged. "Sure."

There were the standard bleachers set up next to the football field, but there were also some next to the pile of brush and sticks that would eventually become the bonfire when the sun went down. We made our way to an empty set of bleachers, but Emma didn't even sit with us. She joined two girls a couple rows down who were both wearing almost identical outfits, except one was pink, and one was yellow. I didn't know either girl by name, but the one in yellow glanced up at me when Emma sat down.

The glance was quick and brutal. I didn't even have time to make a similar face in response.

"Don't worry about them," Bridget said.

"Are we being replaced?" I asked.

Shelby chimed in with, "They're sophomores."

Ah, that would explain it. Emma went and founded her own circle while Bridget and I were on the outs. Emma had always been kind of a strange addition to our friend group. She used to play on the soccer team but quit when we started high school. The last three years, she would rotate in and out, but we always made sure to include her when we were doing group activities. I guess now she was leaving for good.

We watched the game with mild interest and cheered in all the appropriate spots. We greeted other team members and made sure they found spots to sit, especially the freshmen. At one point, Bridget jumped down to herd new players, which was technically not her job anymore, but I guess old habits die hard.

We still hadn't elected a new captain yet. I assumed Joely was waiting until the season officially started, so the new girls could get to know the team a little bit before votes were cast.

I was getting thoroughly bored when Bridget brushed past me, and her knuckles brushed against mine, feather-light.

If I hadn't been watching her every move and flip of her wispy blonde hair, I might have missed the touch. I watched her saunter off into the semi-darkness, away from the bright stadium lights. I waited for one breath and then slid off the bleachers and slunk after her.

The baseball diamond was separated from the football field by the track, bleachers, and a swath of well-trod grass. I saw Bridget slip through the gate and disappear into a dugout. I threw a quick glance over my shoulder to ensure we weren't being followed before squeezing through the gate.

"It's dark as fuck," I said.

I heard a giggle, and then my arm was almost tugged out of my socket as she pulled me into the dugout and plopped me on a bench.

"Shut up."

Bridget straddled my lap, and my breath caught, and my pulse ratcheted up.

"It's dirty in here."

"That's why you're on the bench." Her face was close to mine, but I could still only barely make out her features and her clever Cheshire grin. "Cause you're wearing pants."

Her hands came up to cradle my face, and mine landed on the backs of her thighs. They were warm, even though the August night air had turned chilly.

She kissed me, the press of her lips soft and unhurried. Kissing Bridget was like nothing I'd ever experienced in my life. I tried to focus on the kiss and ignore the happiness blooming in my chest and the urge to smile against her.

"Bridget, Soph, are you—"

The happiness bubble burst.

I hadn't heard anyone approach, but I was otherwise occupied and not listening for eavesdroppers.

Bridget managed to get halfway off my lap; her knee had collided hard with the wooden bench when we heard Emma's voice. We both looked to the doorway. Emma was standing there, phone held out like a flashlight, one hand on the side of the dugout, one foot still leading as if she'd stopped in her tracks.

And I imagined she had.

"Gross."

The condemnation slipped from her mouth almost without thought. I could tell because she looked shocked that she'd said anything at all, and her cheeks flushed darkly.

I could understand the knee-jerk reaction. A lifetime of church and Sunday school tends to indoctrinate one. Also, I don't think there was any way to platonically explain away the scene before her.

"Um, hey," I said.

Emma turned on her heel and fled.

"Well, fuck." Bridget slid the rest of the way off my thigh and pulled out her phone, flipping it open to shine on her knee. The skin was scraped raw and leaking blood.

"I hope your tetanus shots are up to date."

She gingerly touched the edges of the wound and sighed, heavy and resigned.

I couldn't presume to know what she was thinking but imagined it went something like, *Well, shit, we are so royally screwed. Here comes the damnation and hellfire.*

I kept my hands to myself because I wasn't sure if she wanted to be touched anymore. Not when she sat there so quiet and fatalistic. She'd had a lot longer to think about coming out than I had, and I was sure this was not on her list of top ideas. I had also already lived through a reputation-ruining public scandal. I was kinda immune. I slowly crossed my arms over my chest and waited as she fiddled with the edges of her scrape.

"I'm sorry," she said finally. "I didn't mean to drag you into my shit."

"Um, excuse me." This time I did grab her hand. "I believe I jumped into your shit willingly."

That got a quick smile.

"Do you think Emma's going to say anything?"

"I honestly don't know."

I didn't hear any extra commotion coming from the direction of the bonfire or football field. So maybe that meant Emma had gone back to her new friends and hadn't revealed what she'd seen...yet. I couldn't imagine it was a secret she would be able to keep for long. But maybe we could get to her first.

Bridget's fingers threaded through mine. "What are we going to do?"

I had several ideas, one of which included cornering Emma and threatening her within an inch of her life to keep her mouth shut.

"Whatever you want," I said instead.

I got home from the bonfire way later than my suggested curfew, but that didn't seem like a battle Dad bothered with fighting anymore.

I assumed they would both be asleep, seeing as it was one in the morning.

Imagine my surprise to find my mom sitting on the edge of my bed, Sir Bearington clasped in her lap.

I really wished my parents would stop surprising me in the dark. My heart was not going to be able to handle it if they kept this up.

I braced myself with a hand on the edge of the doorjamb. "Uh, Mom, sorry I'm so late. I was just with Bridget at the bonfire. You know, at school." The apology came tumbling out of my mouth before I really had time to think about it. She knew where I was. I also conveniently reeked of bonfire smoke.

She was in matching floral pajamas and stroked Sir Bearington's head absently. "I knew where you were." She smiled. "I'm glad you and Bridget made up. Friendships can be hard, sometimes."

Well, that was an understatement.

Bridget and I had talked several times about telling our parents, and neither of us had reached a firm conclusion yet. I wanted to tell my mom so bad, it was a constant pain in my chest. It felt like I was always lying to her by omission. But I worried. Would she look at me differently? Would she love me differently? Would I be able to survive that?

There was a slim chance she might hear about it anyway since we had decided on was to beat Emma to the punch at school. Neither of us wanted to live under the shadow of gossip and rumors as we waited for the news to drop.

Bridget had scoured our Code of Conduct several times over the summer for anything remotely prohibiting same-sex fraternization and came up empty-handed. Which meant there was nothing the school could do to us. Except maybe call our parents again.

I went to sit beside her on the bed, leaning into her shoulder. She smelled like her favorite scent—clean and airy.

She wrapped an arm around my shoulders.

I thought about Emma. "Yeah, friendships can be hard."

I felt her nuzzle the top of my head. "Sophia, you know if there's something going on, you can talk to me. I might not understand what really happened between you and Bridget, but you can still tell me."

I sighed. I wanted to tell her the truth so bad. Fear kept it bottled in. "You know I don't really have a sex list, right? And the picture of Father Adrian, it was just...stupid. Nothing happened."

She chuckled. "Honey, if I thought something had happened, I would have gone to talk to the police and not your principal."

Well, it was good to know my mom didn't think I was a slut.

"Honey, listen." She ran her hand down my hair. "I know you teenagers think y'all are the first people ever to be teenagers, but I was your age once too. I know what high school feels like. I know what the hormones and the emotions feel like."

Yeah, but did she know what it felt like to fall for her best friend?

Mom was still talking. "I know things can feel catastrophic sometimes. But it's almost over, and then you get to go make stupid decisions in college. I just want you to be safe and be smart. And I wouldn't care if you did have a list. The number of people you sleep with means absolutely nothing."

I raised my eyebrows even though she couldn't see my face, interest piqued.

Where had she come by such an opinion? I was suddenly very curious about my mom before she became my mom.

It took a couple moments of thinking about my mom in college before I realized she had said *people* and not *boys*.

My heart thudded in my chest.

Did she know?

Was she trying to tell me she knew?

"Sophia?"

"Do you mean it?" I asked. "I can tell you anything?"

I felt her tense against me, and I could almost hear her running down a list of horrible things I could possibly reveal. What would be the worst?

She wrapped her other arm around me, Sir Bearington squished between us, and squeezed me hard. So hard it almost hurt. But I needed this. Needed to feel that she had my back, no matter what, even if I couldn't tell her everything yet.

She pressed her face into the top of my head. "Yes, my sweet girl. Anything."

TWENTY-TWO
August 2006

THE FIRST DAY OF senior year dawned bright and pretty, like a dream. Or a nightmare if you happened to be a vampire.

I had stayed up late prepping for this day. All my laundry was done, polos crisp and unstained and hung up in my closet, skirt pleats neatly ironed. I had even cleaned up my desk, clearing off old scraps of paper and broken charcoals, making neat little stacks of supplies instead. Mom asked me if I was feeling sick and pressed the back of her hand against my forehead.

My soccer bag for practice after school was packed—I even had clean socks—and I had made my own lunch. The neatness and preparedness were out of character for me, but I needed things to do to keep my mind off the day. Not that it helped much. No amount of cleaning could erase the nervous rumbling in my gut.

I'd woken up to a text from Bridget: *Are you ready?*

I was tempted to reply with *no, what the hell are we doing*, but sent an enthusiastic string of hearts instead. We had discussed this and agreed. If she had enough nerve, then so did I.

After my shower, I texted again: *balls of steel*

Her reply: *Lol love you*

My stomach leaped up into my throat. It was a sensation that felt like falling and not knowing if anyone was going to catch you or if you were going to end up a flat, squished pancake on the ground.

But maybe I was overthinking things. It wasn't the first time we'd said I love you. But something felt different this time because she wasn't just my friend. Was it an I love you, friend, because you're just so cute and quirky? Or was it an I love you, you, because you're the person that I kiss? I decided to leave that quandary to deal with later. Before I broke a sweat and messed up my straight hair.

I put my phone and sketchbook in my soccer bag. I had spent way too much time illustrating the inside of the front cover in preparation for my AP Art class. Bridget had tried to convince me to come over and label and organize my supplies for my other classes—like she did. She had printed out labels that proudly read *Bridget M. James, Senior* that she could stick on all her notebooks, folders, pencil case, and all the other crap she needed. I refused to be that excited about school. The only things I cared about were my art portfolio and maybe being scouted for a college team.

Dad was in the kitchen when I entered, bag slung across my chest. He was frying eggs on the stove and gave me a quick, warm smile. Mom had already left for work.

"Cheesy scrambled eggs, coming right up!"

There was only one place set at the bar: a small plate, fork, and glass of chocolate milk.

I glanced at the clock on the stove. I was early. I probably had some wiggle room for breakfast. It would be the first time I ate breakfast before school in years.

He sprinkled shredded cheese over the pile of eggs, folded them together to melt the cheese, and scooped them out over my plate.

"Thanks, Dad." I didn't sit but grabbed the fork and shoved some bites in my mouth.

"So, first day of school, huh?" With my mouth full, I nodded. "Are you excited?"

I swallowed. "Yeah, I guess so. It's just school." And excited wasn't the word I would use to describe my current feelings.

"Do you have any colleges picked out? We should take some time to go on school visits."

I choked on my eggs. "Dad." It was 7:15 in the morning. I had bigger fish to fry, and honestly, I had never thought I would be going on college visits with my formerly absentee father. One of my classes had gone on a college visit sophomore year, and I had always assumed I'd either be going with my friends or my mom.

"Well, just think about it."

Now that senior year had dawned, I was sure Mom wouldn't let me quit thinking about it. She had been bugging me to retake the ACT and try for a higher score, but I was banking on an athletic scholarship anyway.

"I will. Thanks for the eggs."

He gave me a small wave out of the kitchen.

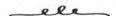

Our plan was a simple one.

The first bell didn't ring until 7:52, so the student body gathered in the gym to wait. Bridget was seated in the middle of the soccer team; they were easy enough to spot as we tended to segregate voluntarily by grade level and/or extracurricular activity. I recognized a gaggle of new freshmen from the summer tryouts. Shelby was leaning up against Bridget's shins as I sauntered up, pulling at my skirt to make sure my bag hadn't hiked it up inappropriately.

Shelby looked up from the book on her knees. "Good morning, sunshine! You're early. Don't you usually stroll in during first period?"

Bridget and I locked eyes. "I'm turning over a new leaf." She and I had first period together this year, and our plan wouldn't work if I were late.

"Are you reading a textbook?"

Shelby carefully marked her place with a piece of notebook paper. "Just trying to get a head start."

"Nerds."

I didn't get a chance to join them on the bleachers because just then, the bell let out its loud, sharp shriek that made several people jump. That tended to happen if you weren't paying attention to the time.

Sister Constance was at one of the entryways with a three-foot ruler hollering, "Walk, do not run!" Honestly not even sure how she was still allowed to work in a school.

Joely was in charge of one of the entryways as well, looking immaculate in her sleek Nike tracksuit, curled up-do, and pearl studs. We shuffled past her with a chorus of "Coach, coach, coach," and she gave Bridget and I a meaningful look that I could only interpret as *Behave*.

Bridget and I headed toward the hallway where the senior lockers were assigned. Thankfully, I got to start fresh this year and didn't have to live with the faint reminder of WHORE. I heard they tried to scrub the spray paint off, but it just left a faded patch that was still unfortunately legible. Then they tried repainting the lockers, but the colors didn't quite match, so you could still tell which one used to be mine. My condolences to whichever junior ended up with that one.

Bridget dropped her stuff off first, and then we migrated to my locker, bidding farewell to Shelby in the process.

For first period, we had decided on a music theory class that was taught more like a music appreciation class, and I heard they mostly watched *Amadeus*. It was supposed to be a fluffy elective so I could survive AP Art and Bridget could survive AP Bio, Lit, and Government.

She had her gigantic doorstop of a Biology textbook pressed up against her chest as she watched me stuff my soccer bag into my locker. I pulled out my sketchbook and the one other notebook I'd be using for everything else. I stuck a pen into the fluffy, messy bun on top of my head.

"Are you ready?" she asked. One hand had released the textbook and was held out between us, expectant.

My stomach roiled, and I could feel the heat creeping up my neck. With a short exhale of breath, I reached out and grabbed her hand. Maybe a little too forcefully.

She smiled, huge and radiant and genuine, and I felt her squeeze my fingers. The cacophony of milling students died away, and it was just me and her.

I was going to walk down the senior hallway and into that first period classroom hand-in-hand with my best friend, my friend-who-was-a-girl, but also so much more.

I touched the heart charm at my throat and grinned.

Thank you for reading *The Girls of Fall*!

Reviews are a great way to support authors, and I would appreciate you leaving one on the site where you bought the book!

xoxo jessica

PLAYLIST

The following is a small sampling of songs that make up an almost ten-hour playlist that I would listen to while thinking about and writing *The Girls of Fall*.

"betty" - Taylor Swift

"Bring Me To Life" - Evanescence

"Fall In Line" - Christina Aguilera, Demi Lovato

"Know Your Name" - Mary Lambert

"Too Young" - Sabrina Carpenter

"Joanne" - Lady Gaga

"Salvation" - Gabrielle Aplin

"Quit Playing Games (With My Heart) - Backstreet Boys

"Sinners" - Lauren Aquilina

"Girlfriend" - Avril Lavigne

"Boyfriend" - RaeLynn

"First Love" - Adele

"Problem" - Natalia Kills

"Red" - Taylor Swift

"Black Sheep" - Gin Wigmore

"Young" - Kenny Chesney

"If I Loved You" - Delta Rae, Lindsey Buckingham

"Dirty Little Secret" - The All-American Rejects

"Hurricane" - Halsey

"Girl Next Door" - Saving Jane

ABOUT THE AUTHOR

Jessica Minyard (she/her) is an author, poet, small YouTuber, higher ed professional, Sagittarius, and boy mom. She lives in Kentucky with her family.

She has an MFA from Lindenwood University and her short fiction and poetry has appeared in *Flash Fiction Magazine*, *Vamp Cat Magazine*, *salt + vinegar zine*, *Nightingale and Sparrow*, *Re-Side Zine*, *Taco Bell Quarterly*, *Kaleidotrope*, and elsewhere.

You can find her on Twitter and Instagram as @callmeshashka or on her YouTube channel.

To stay connected and keep up with her work, sign up for her newsletter: https://www.subscribepage.com/jessicaminyard.

Made in the USA
Monee, IL
02 January 2022